BUILDING
WAVES

OTHER WORKS IN DALKEY ARCHIVE PRESS'S
JAPANESE LITERATURE SERIES

Embracing Family
Nobuo Kojima

Realm of the Dead
Uchida Hyakken

The Budding Tree: Six Stories of Love in Edo
Aiko Kitahara

The Temple of the Wild Geese and Bamboo Dolls of Echizen
Tsutomu Mizukami

The Glass Slipper and Other Stories
Shotaro Yasuoka

The Word Book
Mieko Kanai

Isle of Dreams
Keizo Hino

Plainsong
Kazushi Hosaka

The Shadow of a Blue Cat
Naoyuki Ii

Flowers of Grass
Takehiko Fukunaga

TAEKO TOMIOKA

BUILDING WAVES

TRANSLATED BY LOUISE HEAL KAWAI

DALKEY ARCHIVE PRESS

CHAMPAIGN • DUBLIN • LONDON

Originally published in Japanese as *Namiutsu Tochi* by Kodansha, Tokyo, 1983

Library of Congress Cataloging-in-Publication Data

Tomioka, Taeko.
[Namiutsu tochi. English]
Building waves / by Taeko Tomioka ; translated by Louise Heal Kawai. -- 1st ed.
   p. cm.
ISBN 978-1-56478-715-6 (pbk. : alk. paper)
I. Kawai, Louise Heal. II. Title.
PL862.O38N313 2012
895.6'35--dc23
                              2012001867

Partially funded by a grant from the Illinois Arts Council, a state agency

This book has been selected by the Japanese Literature Publishing Project (JLPP), an initiative of the Agency for Cultural Affairs of Japan

The translator would like to thank Anna Husson Isozaki for all her advice and insight during the editing process and beyond.

www.dalkeyarchive.com

Cover: design and composition by Sarah French
Printed on permanent/durable acid-free paper and bound in the United States of America

1

Back when I used to watch a lot of prime-time TV, there was a particular dating game show that always caught my attention. At first the young men and women were divided by a wall, and each had to imagine what the other was like only from their voice. Then when the host yelled out "Time to Meet!" the divider would be raised, and the couple would have their first conversation face to face. This conversation invariably kicked off with one member of the couple asking the other, "What do you do in your spare time?" As I watched week after week, I heard the same old question over and over. Eventually, I was sick of hearing it. But there was no denying it was a good way of getting to know something of the other's private life or personal side.

"What do you do in your spare time?"

"Hmm, I guess I go for drives and stuff."

"Oh, you're into cars?"

"Yeah. You too?"

"Yeah."

When I was a student in the sixties, no one in my circle of friends had a driver's license. I know that kids nowadays all go to driving school in the summer vacation of their first year in college, but still a response like "I go for drives and stuff" irritated me to no end.

What exactly is *someone's personal life . . . ?*

"So what do you do in your spare time?" I asked.

I found it amusing that I had resorted to the same line of questioning as the young people on the dating game show. At the same time, I reasoned that this line of questioning might just be a universally-accepted, logical approach to getting to know someone.

"Let me see . . . mostly I just drive around."

"Oh, in your car."

Right then, in the beginning, I wasn't remotely interested in learning any more about this man's private life. I mean, we weren't anywhere near a car and I didn't see any connection between the man and the concept of driving, or even to a car. Nowadays, being able to drive a car is nothing out of the ordinary. But I suppose I have to admit that, for me, there was still something special about it.

And so, when the man had finally turned up in his car, I was momentarily dazzled by the combination of this meticulously cared-for vehicle and the man behind the wheel.

"About how much does a car cost?" I asked.

"Well, it depends. The most expensive can go for just about anything. This one cost me one and a half million yen."

"Hmm, that's pretty expensive."

"It's just an average car."

"A car's something you'd buy on credit, right?"

"Yes, normally. But I paid for this one in cash. My financial controller is generous about those sorts of things."

I didn't own a car and couldn't drive, which put me pretty much out of touch with today's society—a fact I was well aware of. It was only someone like me—unable to operate what had become an everyday piece of equipment—who would think it so special. But it did turn out that through his flippant use of the term *financial controller* to refer to his wife I had managed to uncover a tiny bit more of this man's personal life.

"Expensive, though, aren't they—cars? Or maybe I'm just cheap. Perhaps career women are all cheap by nature," I said jokingly. But the man took me at my word.

"It must be really difficult for you women to have a career—unless you've got your husband's understanding anyway," he replied, a serious expression on his face. The moment I heard him use the phrase *your husband's understanding*, I immediately tried to forget he'd said it. What exactly was a husband supposed to understand? Whenever Japanese wives say to each other "You're so lucky to have your husband's understanding," the phrase always sounds empty, as so many clichés do. But I don't doubt that if I turned to the speaker, the kind of person who thoughtlessly tosses around that kind of expression, and told them how meaningless it was, they wouldn't have a clue what I was talking about. I had scant tolerance for any of these kinds of platitudes, so when the man said "your husband's understanding," I was so busy trying to keep talking, to hide how much it bothered me, that I got all flustered.

If we'd been on that game show, the red, heart-shaped lamp that signaled a successful match would never have lit up. It only took a couple of minutes in the man's car for me to come to this conclusion. The man, for his part, seemed totally bewildered by my conversation.

"This is the first time I've ever talked to an intellectual woman like you," he commented.

I laughed. "Look, I wrote a few poems when I was younger. Really, the word *poet* is an overstatement. I was more like a disreputable hack. I wasn't earning any kind of honest living—I was a reprobate, scum of the earth . . ." I was laughing but I realized he was staring at me blankly, uncomprehending. This wasn't a look of reproach for my fake badass routine—it was all too obvious that he'd just never heard the terms *hack* or *reprobate*.

"But I've seen books of your poems in the bookstore. If you've been published then you must be an intellectual," the man persisted, apparently in earnest.

"Is that right?"

"Sure it is," he grinned triumphantly.

There being nothing more to say on the subject, I instead grabbed a box that was sliding around on the back seat.

"Are there tapes in here?"

"Do you want to listen to something?"

"What kind of music do you have?"

"*Song of the Seasons, Song of Daybreak*, you know—traditional folk songs. That kind of thing."

"Huh?"

"Shall I put one in?"

"Um . . . I'm fine, thanks."

Without warning, he launched into a rendition of *The Seashore Song*. His powerful tenor voice, exactly what you'd imagine springing forth from a large body like his, resonated through the car. He didn't seem to put much effort into each note, yet there was volume to spare. His rich, hearty voice never seemed to crack or falter.

"You're in a good mood," I remarked.

"Of course. I never get to go for a drive with a woman next to me," he replied seriously, then resumed his song.

I looked over at him. "You must be at least six feet tall."

"Right. Six feet two inches."

"And about 180 pounds?"

"More than that."

"I'm guessing you've never had any serious illness."

"No, never. The past few years I haven't so much as caught a cold."

"That's probably because you don't poison your body with stuff like this," I grinned, lighting a cigarette.

"Right. I don't drink and I've never even tried smoking."

"Perfect health."

For the past month, I'd had a constant headache. From the middle of my forehead, around past my temples, to behind my ears, it felt as if my head was being squeezed by an iron band. There seemed to be no way of loosening it.

The Seashore Song continued. In that wholesome, crystal-clear tenor. He spun the wheel with arms that looked sturdy and strong. He hadn't made a single lighthearted comment the whole time we'd been together, but I assumed that *The Seashore Song* was his way of communicating his good feelings. He was entirely contained in his own bubble of healthy wholesomeness, completely indifferent to how bored I was. You couldn't really call him overweight, but he was bulky, like one of those sixth-grade winners of a school fitness contest. You'd see their photos in the local newspaper, bursting with energy and vitality. They always reminded me of samurai warrior action figures. His hair was cut short too, like a professional athlete's, a pair of glasses the only distinguishing mark on his untroubled face. Even these weren't particularly thick, so they didn't obscure his cheerful expression in any way.

"Don't you like any popular songs? How do you feel about jazz or rock?" I asked in the face of the interminable *Seashore Song*.

"It's not that I don't like them. I just can't sing them. That vibrato sound—like the one you get in *enka* songs—I just can't get it right. Whenever I try to sing that way, people tell me to stick to folk songs."

"That's unusual for a Japanese person. Unless you're very young. Usually if a Japanese person tries to sing a foreign song, any song really, somewhere along the way, that vibrato creeps in and it turns into *enka*. Well, at least with the over-forty crowd."

I grinned, knowing that he was forty-two. However, he chose not to show his solidarity with his generation and said simply, "I just like folk songs."

That was a total conversation killer if ever I'd heard one. There was nothing to do but pass the time by talking; hopefully I could entertain the man and at least amuse myself doing it. It had plainly escaped his notice that providing what amounted to some kind of one-way chatting service was my only source of entertainment here with him. It wasn't taking me long to work out that he wasn't the kind of person who liked to strike up a conversation, or even considered it a way for two people to have a good time together. I had to abandon all hope of that.

But really, I decided, it wasn't that he was taciturn by nature, or shy, or even inarticulate. I concluded, rather maliciously, that he just didn't have anything to say. Oh well, I supposed it was probably better than having to sit there bored, nodding in agreement while he tried to explain mundane concepts that most people already understood (such as the term *vibrato*) in an interesting or amusing way.

Normally if two strangers want to get to know each other better, there's really no alternative to conversation. You can try joking around the whole time, but that method only works with some people. And there's a point at which bland, neutral small talk is no longer enough—without asking about each other's personal life, there's really no other way of getting to know someone. So, in most cases, you chat casually about your hobbies, work, or family, and in turn listen to the other person chatting about the same things. In other words, it is a straight exchange; you offer information about yourself and acquire information about the other party in return.

I had believed that most human beings possessed this basic knowledge of the etiquette of discourse, and knew how to employ it to make pleasant conversation. This man possessed none of that. When I asked him what he did for a living, he replied that he was a salaryman, or salaried worker. When I asked him if he worked for a trading company, he simply said, "Nothing that exciting."

"A government office?"

"No."

His replies were so terse that outside of naming every occupation under the sun, I was never going to get anywhere. So I gave up. The only question he had given a clear-cut answer to was the price of his car. Maybe I should assume that this was the one area of his life he was confident about.

Still, little by little, I had come to know more about this man's personal life. Using a mixture of imagination and guesswork, I had filled in the details around the little information I had, and constructed in my head a more or less full portrait of who he was . . .

Every morning he wakes up and descends the stairs from his apartment on the fifth floor of a concrete-block building. This concrete box had originally been painted cream or a whitish gray, but as ten or maybe twenty years have passed, it has turned steadily darker. Here and there linger yellowing lines, testifying to where cracks in the outer walls have been filled in. As he leaves for work, the soles of the man's shoes echo loudly in the narrow stairwell.

In the middle of the "village" created by row upon row of identical concrete boxes stands a bus stop. Up until three years ago, the man used to commute by riding this bus for thirty minutes to the nearest train station. Now that he has joined the growing tribe of car owners, he climbs into his beautiful, cream-colored, unblemished car (I admit that's a strange adjective to apply to a car) and drives himself to work.

Any concrete-box village has parking spaces between each box with a whole array of different colored cars in a line. Each of the boxes consists of four or five floors, with many apartments on each floor, meaning the inhabitants' dwellings are squeezed together into one cramped space. Each dwelling is made up of several small rooms. The one inhabited by this man consists of two small bedrooms, one tiny living area and an only slightly roomier kitchen-dining room, along with a single bathroom and separate toilet—a total floor space of just under six hundred square feet. The rent is about twenty thousand yen a month. He says it's too inexpensive to ever consider moving. I suppose that's not an unreasonable attitude . . .

This was all I knew (including the embellishments I'd added from my imagination) of the living environment of this man who never revealed anything of his private life. My imagination had been spurred into action not so much by my curiosity, but by the fact that he behaved too much like some airhead girl who never really has an opinion about anything, and I've always wanted to squish those kinds of people like bugs. It turned out he wasn't hiding anything interesting, nor was he secretly a prince pretending to be a pauper; he was nothing more than a regular apartment dweller. If only he'd mentioned the K—— apartment complex in the first place, everything would have been simpler.

I was already familiar with the K—— complex. It stood on top of a hill overlooking K—— yato, which was an old word for valley. It wasn't only K——, but within the sprawling M—— City area there were many other place names that ended in -*yato*. Five years ago, when I first moved to this area, I was amazed when I looked at a map and found how many place names had this suffix. All these places were situated between hills. The frequency of the suffix *yato* testified to how hilly the land was in this region.

I lived several hills away from the K—— apartment complex. The local terrain featured both high and low hills, and I lived on one of the lower ones. But high or low, homes had been built on the slopes of these hills and people had come to live in them. The valleys too were chock-full with them. In the M—— City vicinity, there were numerous apartment complexes like the K——, and their population was constantly increasing.

There had never been any question that the person this man called his "financial controller" was his wife. In most Japanese families, the woman is in charge of the household budget, so it wasn't too unusual of a title. That expression had even been popular at one point. At the same time, though, there was a whiff of something underhanded and ingratiating in the title. By handing over his full salary to his wife and having her run the household completely, the man was also absolving himself of any responsibility for financial problems. The flip side of complete trust is total dependence. In the matter of household finances (actually, it's not only limited to finances) many men treat their wives like a mother and play the role of little boy. That might be okay inside the home, but I wondered just how appropriate it was to use the phrase "my financial controller" and reveal that kind of relationship to outsiders.

This same wife also descends the concrete stairs every day on her own way to work. She takes the bus from the apartment village to the local station, changing trains twice. It takes her almost two hours to reach her office in the city. Every morning at five A.M. she gets up to prepare breakfast, then at six she and her husband eat together. The wife takes the concrete stairs first, at about five minutes to seven. Half an hour later, the husband climbs into his car. It takes him about twenty-five minutes to get to work. In the early evening, the husband gets home first at around four thirty. The wife arrives at the local train station at six. She does the shopping, then gets home around seven P.M., and starts on dinner. The two of them eat around eight. Afterwards, the wife cleans up, washes the dishes, and at nine thirty or ten P.M. finally falls into bed. The husband stays up until eleven watching TV. Except for weekends and holidays, they never deviate from this timetable. Every day without fail, you could set your watch by the sound of the wife's footsteps, then the husband's footsteps echoing in the stairwell.

"Don't you ever make dinner while you're waiting for your wife to come home?"

"No. She doesn't like me to."

Since meeting me, the man's timetable had started to vary slightly. He had some free time between four thirty and seven P.M. That became the time for our secret trysts. Well, I say trysts, but it was nothing more than driving around in his car, just as he always did in his spare time. I'd tried all sorts of things to try to loosen that iron band around my head. Now, clutching at straws, I had decided to hitch a ride as he went about doing his favorite thing, "just driving around."

The "around" was, more specifically, the rolling hills of the region. Dotted here and there among the hills and valleys were sites where remains from the late Stone-Age Jomon period had been discovered. Adjacent to one of these sites stood a tiny community cultural center that served as a kind of museum. Inside, I'd seen a panoramic model of the whole area around M—— City, showing all its hills and valleys. Viewed from above, the undulating land rippled like the waves of some great ocean. It wasn't difficult to imagine how, thousands of years ago, human beings had noticed that these sunny hills overlooking flat and lush, suitably water-retaining valleys were an ideal habitat, and had decided to settle here. As the man and I drove along the asphalt roads that cut across the hills and the almost overly wide roads that swept through the valleys, then navigated the steep ups and downs of the roads passing through residential neighborhoods, the waves of the panoramic model from the museum came to life.

"Without a car I could never have been able to get way out to a place like this," I said, gratefully.

I was the kind of person who always walked if possible, and had been totally left behind by the new car culture.

On our way home, I spotted something familiar. "Look, isn't that D—— Park? I've been here before. It takes over an hour on foot from my place." In response, the man drove into an almost deserted, weed-filled lot marked *Parking for D—— Park Only.*

D—— Park had a large lake and I'd heard that it was absolutely stunning when the irises or the plum trees were in bloom. It had been during the New Year's vacation several years ago that I'd decided on a whim to pick up a map and take a walk around the area, eventually ending up here.

"Hey, aren't there people in that car? I'm sure I saw somebody in there. What are they doing in the middle of a parking lot like this?"

"Looks like they've got the seats tipped back. They're up to something," he replied.

"Aha! I get it—you tip the seats back. Yeah, right, it looks like a couple of kids. So when you say they're up to something . . ."

The man rolled his eyes as if to say I was a bit slow to catch on. I really knew nothing about the culture of car ownership.

It was early evening and still light, but the park gate was locked.

"So you can do that in a car! I'm beginning to see that a car can be very versatile." I was impressed.

"I thought it was open until six in the summer," the man remarked, completely indifferent to my veneration of car culture.

"I'm getting thirsty. Can we get something to drink?" I asked.

"There aren't any cafés around here—just family restaurants." This was an English phrase I had never heard before.

"What's a *family restaurant*?"

We took a short drive, to a glass-sided, octagonal building by the side of the highway. The man drove into the huge adjacent parking lot. The words *In* and *Out* in English indicated the entrance and exit. It wasn't the first time I'd seen this restaurant's name—I'd read it from bus or taxi windows. I realized it was probably a chain.

"I get it. If you're in a car, you need a place to park. If we'd spotted a coffee shop we wouldn't be able to park there—so they designed places like this for the car enthusiasts. So that's why these kinds of places have been popping up all over recently," I said, once again filled with admiration.

While I had been impressed by all sorts of things, I had managed to forget the iron band around my head, but unfortunately, this man's free time was almost over.

"It feels like America in here," I remarked as we were shown to our seats. It wasn't just that everyone around us was eating hamburgers and drinking Coke—it was the atmosphere, like a typical roadside diner in an American movie. The faces of the other customers, sleepily sipping their Cokes, reminded me of the young boy and girl I'd glimpsed through the car window in the parking lot at D—— Park. I looked over the menu, complete with color photos of the offerings.

"I'm hungry, but I don't really feel like a burger. I'll have coffee and a slice of chocolate cake," I said, noting that even a child who hadn't learned to read yet would have no problem ordering with these large, vivid photos next to the list of choices.

"I'll have the same."

"Aren't you hungry?"

"I guess I am."

"So why don't you have something more?" I suggested, but then remembered he'd be going home and eating dinner at eight o'clock.

"Do you ever go out to this kind of place with your wife?" I asked.

"Sometimes on the weekend I ask her if she wants to go out for coffee, but she always refuses, so I end up just coming and drinking a cup by myself."

"So you never eat out at all?"

"She doesn't want to. She doesn't like going out on her days off."

"I suppose when you have to go out to work every day you feel like staying home when you can," I remarked. "That and there must be laundry and other housework to catch up on."

I couldn't tell whether he couldn't stand being hungry any longer, or he had an enormous appetite, but after polishing off his chocolate cake, he ordered a sandwich. Maybe that's just how it is with men.

"If you eat that much before dinner, you're going to end up getting fat," I teased him.

"Yeah, I guess so," he replied complacently.

2

I wasn't remotely interested in things like the man's heritage or family background, but if I didn't even know what kind of work he did it was pretty difficult to hold a conversation. It might be okay in some romantic movie where the heroes fall in love without even learning the other's name, but I was supposed to be driving around with him for fun. As I was the one who had asked him to let me ride along, I couldn't sit there and pout because it wasn't going my way. At the same time, when the other person didn't have anything to offer to the conversation, I couldn't start grilling him like a police interrogator. While seeming to joke around, I could subtly steer the conversation to coax him into dropping some clues, but not when the other party point-blank refused to cooperate. When he'd given me the brush-off one too many times, I found it difficult to believe it was out of some kind of humility or modesty. When my questions, carefully worded in a roundabout manner so as not to make him feel uncomfortable, were continually batted away like some irritating fly that had landed on his face, I began to believe he was either incredibly dense or just plain rude. Was he too dim-witted to get my jokes? I got worked up enough to begin wondering all this about him. I decided that if he was going to give me so much trouble then I was just going to have to blow his cover and expose his identity myself.

And you know what, I bet it's not even much of an identity. Drop that fake veneer of politeness that you use to pretend to others you're a normal, emotionally healthy individual! I thought as my old, reprobate tendencies came crawling back to the surface.

"So do your children go to T—— High School?" I asked as we drove past its gates on our next excursion. T—— was one of the regional public schools of this hill country.

"No, I don't have any children."

"I don't either. Childless couples are definitely a minority. We minorities are always having to put up with being cross-examined by the majority. Don't you agree? When you're still young, all sorts of people take it upon themselves to comment how you haven't any children yet, and when you get older they ask you why you never had any. They always tell you how lonely you must be."

"Uh-huh."

"It's pretty cruel for an infertile couple. But at least they get the sympathy vote for not being able to have any. It's worse for those of us who could have had children but chose not to. We can't really avoid getting the third degree."

"Uh-huh."

"Some psychology expert wrote that when couples have no kids it means that one or the other of them hates their own parents. When I heard this, I thought there might be some truth in it. Sometimes I hated my parents so much I thought if they hadn't existed I wouldn't have had to be born."

"I guess you could feel that way."

"But without kids and both of you working there must be so much money that you've run out of places to put it. I guess you hide it under the floorboards or something," I said, resorting to jokes again. A response along the lines of "No kidding, we had to build a shed behind our apartment building for all the cardboard boxes stuffed with rolls of banknotes" would have given me something to work with. Then at least we'd have been able to enjoy a silly exchange. But in the presence of this man my words had nowhere to go, and just ran around in endless circles.

"Wow, you don't have to go far before you're right in the mountains," I said. We were following a mountain road, lined on both sides by thick, dark woods. I don't know if it was because I wasn't used to sitting in cars for long periods of time, but my butt was completely numb. I was suddenly overcome with an urgent desire to break free of this confining space, better known as a car, and to walk around freely. Today wasn't the usual four thirty to seven P.M. free time, but a national holiday—a whole day free. The man had invited me to drive with him up to a lake which lay on the border with the next prefecture.

By now, I was utterly sick of driving. It wasn't even the two hours I'd already been stuck in the car today, but after only a couple times driving around, the novelty was beginning to pall.

"How long have you been living in that apartment complex?" I asked.

"It's been about ten years now."

"Did you move there for your job?"

"Yeah, it used to take me about two hours by train and bus from my old place."

"So now, twenty or thirty minutes by car must seem like heaven in comparison. But you said that you'd changed jobs, right?"

"Well, yeah . . ."

"And before . . . ?"

"I was a salaryman before too. But I wanted more holidays. I wanted a summer vacation."

"So now you're a teacher?"

"No."

How long was he planning to bait me like this?

From the mountain road, we could see a group of white buildings high up on the summit of the hill.

"Ah, I heard several of the universities had moved their campuses up here. That one must be Q—— University. It's surprising because it doesn't have the image of being so out in the sticks like this. When you hear the name Q—— you picture a college in a seedy downtown area, don't you? Oh, I hope you're not a Q—— graduate . . ." It should have been obvious that I was fishing.

"That's okay. I'm not. I didn't go anywhere as famous as that. I went to the kind of place where you only need to write your name and examinee ID number correctly to get in."

"Do you mind stopping somewhere?" I asked him.

"But we'll be in F—— City soon."

"Anywhere'll do. I just need to pee."

"Oh I see. Sorry, I'm a bit slow to catch on. My mother was always telling me I'm a bit of a dolt, and, to be honest, I think so too."

"Well, I'd certainly agree that you're not the most considerate person I've ever met." The physical and mental effort required to control my bladder was turning me belligerent.

"Even my wife tells me she doesn't have to worry that another woman might fall for me, because I'm so clueless about women's feelings," he conceded.

He kept driving, all the way to downtown F—— City, and even then, I'm not sure if it was because he couldn't find a parking spot or what, but we kept driving around and around the same few blocks. Whenever he spotted a parking space, it turned out to be privately leased, or a customer-only spot belonging to some beauty salon.

"Look, we only need a parking space if we're both getting out. If it's only me, I can get out anywhere."

"Oh, right, right. But what'll you do all by yourself?"

"I'll go into that café, order a Coke or something, and use the restroom."

"Oh yeah, good idea."

About another hour and a half's drive from the café, we began to glimpse the water of the lake glimmering beyond the trees. I was hoping we could park the car and walk down to the lakeside, but I didn't say anything. It was beginning to look as if making it down to the shore was too demanding a task for a self-proclaimed dolt. And being locked in this tiny automotive prison was becoming hellish for me. The car was moving, but I was immobile, constrained by my seatbelt. The man's proposal to "show me the lake" had apparently meant no more than to furnish me with glimpses of water from the windows of his car.

Normally, the view from a window can be captured by words, in the same way we capture and express our everyday, private thoughts through speech. Our words give expression to what we sense and feel, and gradually language itself becomes enjoyable, something playful. Through language, even that brief glimpse of lake water might sparkle like some magical landscape. But clearly there was no possibility of achieving such a moment here. Whenever I spoke, it was as if my words were sucked down into quicksand and disappeared. This man was a linguistic desert.

"So is this the first time you've been here?" As always, I initiated the conversation.

"I've been once before."

"This far?"

"A girl at work asked me to bring her here once, but we had nothing to talk about. On the way home she said she wanted to stop off somewhere, so we had a coffee and I took her home."

"I bet she had something entirely different from a cup of coffee in mind," I laughed.

"I didn't realize that until much later. See, I'm a dolt."

"She never asked you to take her anywhere again, did she?"

"After that one time she wouldn't even drink a cup of tea with me."

"Not surprising, really."

"I'm such a dolt."

"You're not a dolt or awkward. I just don't think you've got much nerve. You're scared to leave your comfort zone—you know, try new things."

"I'm a dolt. All the young women at work call me 'Mr. Safe.' They don't take me seriously when I tell them I'm really a letch."

"Even the seemingly dumbest of young women is blessed with razor-sharp intuition, so I'm guessing that you really are 'Mr. Safe.' That on your days off you do nothing but drive around in your car is perfect proof. I'm no young woman so I don't think you're safe—I think you just like to play it safe. That first time when we ended up at the same table in the cafeteria at the cultural center and I sat in the seat opposite you, I asked you if you'd like some beer. Your response was something along the lines of 'God forbid!' And when I joked that it was only frogs that drank water with their meals, you used the excuse that your face always flushes red after half a glass. I don't understand what's wrong with flushing red anyway. Even if you're not used to drinking beer with a meal, if a stranger offers you some and she's eating at the same table as you, it doesn't matter whether you actually drink it or not, it's normal to let her pour you even just half a glass. And you know we had at least introduced ourselves by then. I assumed you preferred not to have anything to do with other people, but that's not the case, is it? I thought you disliked that kind of forced ritual and were consciously refusing to participate. But it wasn't really deliberate at all, was it?"

"I was shocked. No one had ever called me a frog before."

"So you were offended?"

"But then I saw how it could be true."

"I only said it as a joke. Has no one ever spoken so directly to you before?"

"No, not really."

"And certainly not a woman, right?"

"No, I suppose not."

"Then as soon as you finished your meal, you stood up and marched right out. I was still drinking my beer, so I was left alone in there after everyone had finished. The other two pairs at our table were married couples so it was understandable that they'd got up and left together. But once you'd put down your chopsticks you didn't waste any time getting out of there, did you? As a woman, I'd hoped that you'd be chivalrous enough to accompany me a little longer. If I'd been in your shoes and the person across from me had been the only one still eating, I'd have sat a while sipping my tea. It wouldn't have been for long. And it wasn't as if we hadn't already introduced ourselves. I don't think what you did was because you were a dolt, as you like to call it. What you did to that girl who came up here to see the lake and suggested you stop off on the way back, that was the same thing. Wasn't it?"

"No, I really am a dolt."

"We came all this way up into the mountains to see a lake, so I had wished we could walk down to the edge of the water. But it turns out I enjoyed seeing just a glimpse of that sparkling water. If you hadn't brought me here today, I might have lived my whole life without a glimpse of that lake. Look, it's getting late. Your wife will be expecting you home for dinner."

"When I go out I never know when I'll be back, so she just eats something early by herself."

"Is that right? Then let's stop off somewhere shall we? But I'm no young woman, so I'll tell you straight—this doesn't mean just a cup of coffee. I mean I want to go to a hotel."

"Won't your husband be worried?"

"The only person who needs to worry about whether my husband is worried is me. It's none of your business."

The car set off on a different route to the one we'd taken to get here. I guessed we were heading for the expressway where there was a concentration of love hotels. Evidently, even a dolt of a man knew where that sacred place lay. Outside it had turned to dusk. I'd been shut away inside this metal box for so long that I no longer felt human, I'd become a part of the machine. As one, we hurtled on towards a different, as yet unknown, space.

3

"Your face was so cute. I looked at that cute face and it didn't matter how intimidating you pretended to be."

After that day, the man used to say this quite frequently. To him, my cute face was some sort of trophy. According to this man, either right before, or right after sex my face always "looked so cute." My trophy cute face was concrete evidence to reassure him of my womanliness. He'd glimpsed beauty in my face (or imagined he'd glimpsed it) and by this he was able to classify me as a real woman. This had been a tremendous relief to him. Even if I said something deep, he was able to remember that I was still a woman. It was only then that the man's nerves began to disappear, he started to unwind, and he was able to stop being overly polite. My cuteness also served to relieve him of one more source of anxiety, something that seemed to cause him a great deal of tension, discomfort, intimidation, and plain horror; namely, that I, the woman, was two years older than he. But in the end, thanks to my cute face the man was able to place me below himself, and feel completely at ease.

"Your face was so cute just then," he'd announce every so often, in the manner of someone brandishing proof of something.

I wasn't particularly surprised by this shift in the man's attitude brought on by his discovery of my "cuteness." It was something I'd expect from the kind of man who used expressions like "your husband's understanding."

I tried joking around, saying "I guess I usually have such a horrible face that it really hits you the few times I look cute," but once he'd got hold of his trophy he wasn't going to let go. For him, the business of repeating the phrase "cute face" didn't lend itself to joking. Whether he'd glimpsed it for a brief moment, or whether it had been a brief illusion, my cute face had become a lucky charm. He carried it with him for good luck, and this meant that he was able to go out with me and even have sex without needing to engage me in conversation. Moreover, since uttering the magic phrase, he was now able to think of the two of us as a couple. Every time we got out of the car and walked side by side, he'd say something like, "You're just the right height. I always wanted to marry someone of about your height."

I'm a little under five feet four inches tall, or about average. The man meant that my height was in perfect proportion to his own. He kept on telling me, "I always wanted to marry someone over five feet three inches but I ended up with someone not even five feet." When I asked him teasingly what he'd do if I were over six feet tall, he replied that there were no such women in existence. In this man's hierarchy of height, a woman under five feet was unsuitable from the point of view of balance. His sizeist attitude was exactly the same as that of young women set on bagging a marriage partner over five feet eight inches. Personally, I hadn't grown to the height of five feet four inches just to create pleasing proportions when walking side by side with this man. It just happened that while I was sleeping, somewhere between my birth and the age of fifteen or sixteen, I reached this height all by myself. Then at around the age of fifteen or sixteen, I was used as a "tall girl," useful only for standing at a volleyball net, blocking opponents' shots or shooting my own team's ball into the enemy zone.

At least now there was some relief from the boredom. Thanks to my cute face, something of the man's personal side was beginning to emerge. As there was no point in trying to converse with the man in words, I now sought to discover this personal side through the language of sex.

To be honest, this wasn't the sequence of events that I would have preferred. If I'd actually been able to communicate with him through regular conversation, if that had been enjoyable enough, I don't know whether I'd have pursued sex or not. But my words had been rejected, and none were offered in return. With a person who cannot handle verbal communication, the only way to reach them is through sex.

Come to think of it though, it might have been the opposite way around. Maybe I did imagine having sex with him the minute I saw him, and if conversation wasn't what I was after, perhaps the tedium that I'd been feeling wasn't surprising after all . . . But still, no one could have expected such an utter lack of communication. Surely a forty-two-year-old man and a forty-four-year-old woman, each of whom has already experienced a marriage, shouldn't be like the young people of nowadays who communicate solely with *Seriously?* and *No Way!* and *Cuuute!* I thought we would have had loads to talk about. I also thought that at forty-two and forty-four, we were of the same generation—an age difference of two years was immaterial to me. There can be great enjoyment derived from just talking, without being distracted by the fact that we were a man and a woman. For these reasons, I had thought I could get to know this man. My plans were certainly not for a romantic relationship. I had thought that he felt the same way.

But in reality, he was obsessed with the fact that he had never gone out with an older woman before. I have no idea where it came from, but all his specifications for the right, the appropriate woman to go out with, these kinds of things seemed to be so ingrained with him that any woman who didn't fit these specifications made him uncomfortable. I learned that being younger than him was the most important stipulation, and being about eight inches shorter was requirement number two. He kept repeating, "You look so young!" which I soon realized was his way of tailoring me to the correct specifications, and necessary to his peace of mind.

Sex is one form of communication between a man and a woman (but of course, that is not its only purpose). For me, sex has often been the natural conclusion to an enjoyable conversation. There have been times when I've been completely satisfied by conversation alone, and others when I've wanted verbal communication to shift or evolve into sexual communication. But with this forty-two-year-old man, neither of these fit the case. There was no verbal communication, so right away I was forced to take a shot at sex.

Later that evening we were lying in a love-hotel bed.

"Are you going away anywhere this summer?"

"We're planning a trip to Hokkaido."

"That sounds fun. I've never been to Hokkaido in the summer."

"It's a package tour. It's just for my wife."

"If you're just traveling within Japan, don't you think it'd be more interesting to go by yourselves?"

"It's such a pain to make plans. A package tour is much easier."

"And cheap too, I suppose."

"Right."

I guessed it must have been the cost. If only he could have told me frankly how expensive trips could be if they weren't done as a package. If he'd just talked about the vacations he'd taken in the past—how they were expensive but how the hotel or the food didn't live up to expectations. Simply to say that for a salaryman like him it wasn't possible to take a really interesting vacation, then we would have had enough to get a discussion going.

I looked up and saw the naked bodies of a man and woman "post-communication" reflected in the ceiling mirror. I could see the man's heavy trunk, fleshy buttocks, and sturdy legs. All of his extra chunk was untoned by any physical work or exercise. He looked larger than with his clothes on. There was the slightest narrowing between his chest and waist, but before you got down to the buttocks, he started spreading again. If you opened your hand as wide as it would go, and grabbed as much as you could, there would still be flesh to spare.

"Look at this flab!" I grinned, watching myself grab hold.

"I used to be thin," he replied, but without an ounce of regret.

"What a chunk!"

I continued pinching his flesh and trying to get a rise out of him, but he couldn't be bothered to stop me. I tried a different tack.

"You really are the kind of person who likes to play things safe," I commented. "You had some reason for wanting to stay at this hotel in particular. I can't believe you drove around the block that many times. And you even waited for a parking space to open up. I'd have tried somewhere else right away."

"I pass this place all the time on my way to and from work. I made up my mind that if I ever had the opportunity to go to a love hotel it had to be this one. It just looked nice."

"You're right, it's not bad."

"You see."

"Even so, I'm surprised at how much business it's doing."

"Well, it's Sunday."

"That's strange."

"Why?"

"Well, everyone's come all the way here by car for the exact same purpose. Why do they need to come all this way out into the middle of some rice field? I wonder what kind of person does that? Not that we're ones to talk, of course."

I guessed that he'd been here once, twice, maybe many times before, and that the familiarity of the place made him feel safe. It didn't matter if he had to wait almost an hour for a room to open up—it had to be this place. No matter that there were numerous similar facilities in the vicinity, for this man it was safety first. For his own sense of security, it was quite normal to stop the car at the side of the road and lie in wait for the neon sign on the opposite side of the street to flash to *vacancies*. Then, finally parked, he climbed out of his car as if he were in his garage at home, casually opened the door to the room and slipped inside. (I hadn't even realized that we wouldn't need a key—that it would be left unlocked for us.) He immediately removed his glasses and took off all his clothes, as if it were all second nature. Then he calmly went off to the shower. It was as if ten years of marriage had given him the confidence that in this case he knew all the correct language. There was no trace of the incompetence he showed in verbal communication. He had the air of a normal, run-of-the-mill forty-two-year-old man. There was nothing of the dolt about him at all.

4

Every second or third day the man would invite me to spend his four thirty to seven P.M. free time with him. A short distance from my house there was an empty lot overrun with grass and weeds. It was right at the end of a narrow street that ran to a dead end, and consequently was used as a free-of-charge parking lot by the local residents. The man would carefully squeeze his car in between all of the haphazardly parked cars and wait for me to arrive. He would always call me thirty minutes before so that I knew he was coming. I worked out that he must call right as he left work. If I couldn't make it that day for some reason, I just had to tell him when he called. Those times, we might agree to meet the next day or the day after that.

One day, about five minutes before the agreed meeting time, I was just getting my shoes on when he rang to cancel. The fact that he sounded for all the world like an unctuous businessman with his choice of, "I'm terribly sorry, but would it be at all possible to reschedule our appointment?" alerted me to the fact that there was probably someone else in earshot. The next time he saw me he explained that he'd been asked to run an errand.

"Don't tell me, I'm guessing that wasn't an order or request from your boss. You probably just volunteered for it. *Oh, that's right on my way home. I'll go!* or something, right? You were probably trying to impress somebody. That's why you canceled on me five minutes before we were going to meet. Some supervisor's wife had asked him to drop something off at her parents' place or something. The guy was probably griping about it to you in private, without thinking, and you fell over yourself to offer to take care of it for him. In other words, you made your boss's personal business more important than your own personal business. The rub is I doubt your boss is going to give you any special thanks for doing it. All that brownnosing never pays off, you know."

"You're right. But how come you got all that?"

"Because you're the kind of guy who's nice to everybody. You're like some kind of good-natured country-western singer. You smile at everybody. If there's a car coming toward you on a narrow street you always stop and wave them through. If we stop at a newsstand to ask the way, you've always got a goofy grin on your face and you're annoyingly polite. It's the same when you pay at the love hotel. You go out of your way to be courteous at a place where most people are trying to be anonymous. The woman at the desk even calls after you to take care. You've got the universal seal of approval from the whole world as a friendly, courteous, wholesome, grinning crooner."

"I guess so."

"So you have a special charm that you put on for strangers?"

"I'm the same at home."

In the end, he never apologized for canceling so suddenly.

"My wife and I, we're always back to back," he said one time, out of the blue.

"What do you mean?"

"We sleep back to back all night."

"Oh, really?"

"She doesn't ever seem to be in the mood."

"Oh, really?"

"And if she's not in the mood, then it isn't much fun, you know, *doing* it."

"I guess not."

I assumed that he was trying to make conversation with me by telling me that he didn't have any of the other kind of conversation with his wife. But this had nothing to do with me and I had absolutely no interest in the topic. I had no desire to hear about his domestic sleeping arrangements. I wasn't interested in hearing about this man's wife, and was indifferent to his status as "somebody's husband." I was concerned only with the man himself. If he had had children, I wouldn't be interested in him as the father of these children either.

"I don't imagine you've ever been like that," he added.

"Me? Been like what?"

"My wife's always been kind of frigid. Even when she was young. No one could ever call you that."

"What do you mean by frigid?"

I mean, I understood that he meant his wife was unresponsive sexually, but just like "your husband's understanding," it was a phrase that had been tossed around so much that it had worn horribly thin. I couldn't understand why a person whose sex drive was not particularly high had to be labeled "frigid." I interpreted his meaning as "My own wife has never particularly liked sex, but from what I've seen of you while we've been having sex, you seem to enjoy it." I noticed that for a man who never really talked, once we got onto the subject of sex, he was gladly offering up generous slices of his personal life.

"I know what you're doing these days, but what did you use to do between four thirty and seven in the evening?" I asked. "You certainly weren't at the supermarket buying your groceries."

"I told you, I'd drive around by myself, or just go home and lie on the sofa watching TV."

"So this is a big change for you."

"It is. But if your husband found out, he'd kill me. Doing this with someone's wife."

"So, you're sleeping with someone's wife are you? Hey, I'm my own person. I'm not meeting you as 'someone's wife.' And for that matter, I'm not thinking of you as 'some woman's husband' either."

In the corner of the hotel room stood a minifridge. The air conditioning was freezing cold. It was probably perfectly adjusted to suit someone engaged in strenuous exercise. I wasn't sure that air could get into this sealed, windowless room. Light bulbs on the walls gave off a bizarre orange glow. The ceiling arched up like the bottom of a boat and was covered with mirrors. *Why mirrors?* I wondered. I supposed it was so you could see your reflections and get turned on even more. You could enjoy the great honor of observing yourselves. It might also work as a device for budding actors to turn this secret room into their personal stage. The actors then become their own audience. Only human beings could come up with such a lonely invention.

One of the most enjoyable topics of conversation between lovers is to reminisce about the beginnings of their love affair. It's like a sort of code that only those two people can understand; something that's fun to decipher. Even if the affair only began a few hours earlier, lovers are already eager to begin retracing it.

However, to recall the first time I met this man was to be reminded of the onset of my urge to attack.

When I happened to be seated at the same table as him, and, as most people would have done in the same circumstances, offered to pour him some beer from the bottle in front of me, this man reacted much as an innocent young maiden of long ago might have, should a gentleman have dared to address her. He turned his head away and gave me a complete brush-off. I was so struck, not by the fact that he didn't want any beer, but at how childish his behavior was, that I couldn't help myself.

"Excuse me, but how old are you?" I had asked.

"Huh? I'm forty-two," he replied automatically, taken off guard by my surprise attack. Then he proceeded to finish up his lunch without another word. I realized he didn't give a damn about me, but now my interest was piqued. His forty-two-year-old juvenile rudeness fascinated me. I didn't think his point-blank refusal was out of any normal human shyness.

I got another bottle of beer out of the hotel refrigerator and poured myself some. Fooling around, I forced my glass up against his lips, and finally he took a sip.

"Now that didn't turn you bright red by the looks of it," I smiled, maliciously.

"It's just me you know—I don't have a problem with a woman drinking at all. I'm always telling my wife 'Baby, you ought to try a sip of beer,'" he replied, apparently unfazed by my attack.

"Aha, so you call your wife *baby* then?"

"Yeah, well she always asks me to call her that. She really likes to be called baby."

"Well, I guess it was originally a term of endearment," I conceded, thinking how it had become more of a put-down these days.

"Really? Anyway, she won't even drink beer."

"So when you have dinner you never want a beer, or sake, or a glass of wine with it?"

"Right. You know, it was my wife who pointed out that because I never drink we could shell out for a car."

"So every weekend you and your wife take turns driving . . ."

"The missus doesn't drive."

"Oh, so you call her *the missus* too?"

"So, even when I go out like this on a weekend, I'm so much better then all those husbands who drink, don't you think? My wife's always telling me how low-budget I am."

Even without being asked, this man was gradually revealing more details of his personal life.

"So your wife actually asks you to call her *baby*?"

"She says she's got no one but her husband to call her that. I've called her that ever since I met her."

"You've been married what, about fifteen years?"

"Yes, it's been fifteen now."

"And you were both virgins," I teased.

"Yes, unfortunately we were."

"You haven't been happy?"

"Well, sort of. My mother was sick and she was living with us. Then she died about six years ago."

"So your wife was caring for your mother and going out to work?"

"Yes."

"That's an impressive load. And she asked you to call her *baby* . . ."

"Yes."

"You'd have to lie to a wife like that. You can hardly tell her the truth about some woman you took to a love hotel."

"My wife couldn't even imagine something like that."

"Oh, I wouldn't be too sure about it. Don't overlook a woman's intuition. If you haven't been found out, either you're the perfect villain and she's incredibly slow, or she just pretends not to know in order to keep the peace."

"She's pretty slow, my wife. She never notices anything."

He always put some thought into what part of the hill country we were going to drive around, but it was always up to me to make all the other decisions. What restaurant to go to, what to eat; he never had any ideas of his own. If I asked him what he wanted to eat, he'd inevitably say, "Anything's fine." I didn't really care that much either, but at least I wanted to avoid what passed for a hamburger at some roadside family restaurant. He would cheerfully wolf one down, though, while I just drank a cup of coffee or tea. It turned out he rarely ever ate out, and he was completely indifferent to what he ate. When we went on longer drives, to the sea or somewhere, I would be the one who suggested going to a French or high-class Japanese restaurant, so naturally I paid. He'd say something like, "What a fancy place. You sure have expensive tastes." He suppressed any tone of reproach in his voice, but there was always a pinch of teasing mixed with self-deprecation and a generous helping of envy in the way he said it.

"Didn't I tell you before, that whenever a hack like me came into money, I'd act like Christmas had come early and eat like there was no tomorrow, but when broke, I'd just drink a glass of water and go to bed?" I'd answer, laughing.

"You know we've got a cafeteria at work. They serve up weird stuff like *oden* fishcakes with bread," he informed me.

"Well, if it tastes okay . . ."

"But you know, it's cheap—only three thousand yen a month," he added.

"Well, then even if they serve up cold tofu with bread, you can't really complain, can you?"

"But *oden* with bread!" he repeated in total disgust.

I was about to say, "Well don't eat there if it's that bad!" but stopped myself.

Either quit eating the stuff, or eat it and shut up, I thought. Don't go around bad-mouthing it to everyone else.

Oden and bread wasn't strange at all. In fact, that was pretty good for around a hundred yen.

If you think it's that weird then laugh it off—after you've shelled out more money for a better meal.

"But who in their right mind would come up with an idea like that?" he said contemptuously.

"You know what, it's not that off-the-wall for a hundred-yen lunch," I replied.

"The guys at work and I are always laughing at the things they come up with."

So I guessed he would sit there in the cafeteria insulting the food, while he polished off his *oden* and bread. The combination was bad enough to sneer at, but not bad enough to turn down. He would go around telling everyone how foul it was while continuing to eat it every day.

Back at the French restaurant, I asked him what he was having.

"I guess I'll have steak. I don't really know anything about French food," he answered, staring blankly at the menu.

You know what, just quit taking the piss out of hundred-yen oden *and bread*, I thought. *We're here at this place because we can afford to spend a hundred times that amount.*

When I was a kid, we didn't even have *oden,* let alone bread. And we never once laughed at our steamed potatoes and plain dumplings in broth.

"Was that good?"

"The best! Well, I say *best* but I suppose that only means something if it's the best out of many, but I've only ever been with two women, so . . ." He was totally hung up on this issue, and his complicated explanation didn't interest me in the slightest. To me, the phrase "the best" had no deeper significance than a sigh or a moan. I wasn't interested in exploring his personality at the moment—all I needed then was to grab a fistful of the part of this man's body necessary for a bit of sexual communication. The thing known as *penis* swelled and expanded inside me. Despite feeling soothed by this *thing*, I was not at all soothed by the existence of the man attached to the other end. As he stroked my hair and neck and back, or my breasts, belly, and genitals, the waves that coursed through me were nothing but my ploy to pull his penis inside me as soon as possible. In fact, I almost found all this extra stimulus offensive.

My sexual desire is something plain and direct and has a short fuse. Men are used to women needing a wide range of foreplay for sexual satisfaction. Or perhaps it's just their fantasy that women need their sex dressed up—they believe that women must be craving all these added extras.

Whenever the man and I got together, there was no pleasurable or witty conversation to be had, so there was nothing left to do but have sex. When I rode in his car, I ended up talking in monologues. When I paused, he didn't even nod—there was nothing but a heavy silence. Eventually making a date with this man was purely for sex. And once the purpose of meeting him became clear in my mind, I was finally able to separate the act of sex from the man himself, because from sex, at least, I could still get some pleasure. During the act, I was able, without any feelings of guilt, to completely cut myself off from the man.

He, too, was in no need of myself for sex. He had never turned to me and asked whether it was good or not. If I shifted my torso or legs, so that I could change the sensation I felt in my clitoris, he would respond immediately by concentrating every last part of his body into his penis. It felt as if he was attempting to squeeze the whole of his fleshy body through one tiny opening.

5

"I got a speeding ticket the other day," he announced proudly.

This was a very unusual conversation opening for him. Apparently, he and his wife were in the habit of visiting her parents once a month, and he had been caught over the speed limit on the expressway. Because of this, he'd had to take time off work to attend a one-day course for traffic-law violators, and seemed to feel it was something to be proud of. These kinds of things rarely ever happened to someone like him.

"I've never done anything that wild before in my life," he told me.

"Was it fun?" I asked.

"I've never driven that fast before."

"So you've never committed a traffic violation before?"

"Never."

"I'm guessing you've never even broken the law. I don't just mean when you're driving, but ever."

He didn't bother to respond. Well, it wasn't as if he was the type to make a drama out of it all. Still, it would have been fun if he'd grabbed my hand or something and said, "Hey, how's this for a traffic violation, holding the wheel with one hand, and a woman with the other?"

"Today I'm properly observing the speed limit."

"You know, it's okay as long as you don't get caught. Look, everyone's passing us."

"They're all breaking the speed limit."

"But they're not being stopped."

"Yeah, but I'm such a dolt."

"I'm sure you'd live."

"It's too risky."

"Your wife's parents seem to have great faith in you."

"Yes, they do. They really trust me. They're very fond of me."

"Apparently. You two sound like the perfect daughter and son-in-law, dutifully visiting them every month. But why did you need to go that fast? Especially someone as careful as you."

"I was just trying to get it over with quickly."

"Have you ever been abroad?"

"Just once."

"Where?"

"England."

"On business?"

"No, a package tour. Last summer."

"How was it?"

"Oh we just trailed around after the guide. All I can say is that I've been."

"Okay, I'm paying, so order whatever you want. This place is run by real Chinese people, so I'm betting it's pretty good."

"I don't know. Go ahead and order for me."

"Just give me an idea of what you like or dislike."

"I've never tried anything besides pot stickers, dumplings, and egg rolls."

"Is it really so difficult to think?"

"What do you expect? I've never been to a restaurant like this before. I have a frugal lifestyle. My mother used to go out to work, but she hated eating outside the house. My wife hates take-out food too."

"Your mother used to work?"

"My father died when I was two. My mother suffered a stroke about the time I started work. I have an older sister, but she'd already left home to get married."

"So your wife was a savior to you then."

"Financially, too, because she worked outside as well."

"Then you really shouldn't be hanging out in motels with random women should you?"

"No, I really shouldn't."

"It's really the depths of betrayal."

I ended up ordering way more food than two people could possibly eat.

"Let's go down to the harbor," I suggested as we headed back to the car. I put my arm around his waist, in imitation of the young couples walking by. He put his arm around my waist.

"I'd love to sail away to a far-off land, wouldn't you?"

"Yes."

"But a ship's no fun if you haven't got money. There's a big difference between the classes of travel on a ship. I once took an overseas cruise. There's a huge gap between first and third class.

I was propositioned by this young blond boy I met on board. He was only twenty years old but I was completely blown away by his maturity. You know I was actually with my husband on that ship. That boy told me that my husband was none of his business. He told me I was the only one who could make the decision. If I needed him to be there when I spoke to my husband, he said he would. Otherwise, he said, any other problems that might arise between my husband and me should stay between my husband and me. I was really impressed by that young man's attitude. I was incredibly moved, but in the end I had to turn him down."

This fictitious tale was supposed to be a message to this man but he didn't get it at all.

"That must have come as a shock to your husband," he said, as if he were the one in shock.

"My husband was very impressed with him too. After that, the two of them used to play shogi together all the time. He really was a charming young man. His sense of humor, the jokes he used to tell . . ."

I began to falter. I had been reminded all of a sudden of how little humor this man possessed. I changed tack.

"Isn't there supposed to be a love hotel shaped like a cruise ship around here? I saw it in some magazine. Seeing as we've come all this way we might as well try it, don't you think?"

"Why do they build weird stuff like that?"

"I think it sounds fun. I wonder whether the inside's like a ship too."

That first time, when he'd hung around for over an hour waiting for a room to open up, that hotel couldn't have been more different from a cruise ship-themed love hotel. Its design was very somber and understated. The entrance was designed so you drove in between a tall rock and some low bushes into the parking area. We entered the building itself through a Japanese-style garden, so that the whole place could easily be mistaken for an expensive Japanese restaurant. Even the *vacancies* sign was hidden behind the rock, so that the whole place had a very discreet and demure feeling about it. The kind of man who liked that kind of innocuous appearance and bland atmosphere was hardly likely to dig a trashy, ocean liner-shaped sex palace.

As we approached, the big, thick funnel of a massive ocean liner appeared, towering above the low-roofed houses. The view was surreal. The avant-garde architects of the sex industry had anchored an enormous ship on the land—practically in people's backyards.

"What an amazing view," I said with genuine admiration, but the man wasn't looking at the ship.

"I heard that there's a young French architect who came to Japan and decided to study buildings like this," I continued, undaunted. "He claims they're the most interesting structures in Japan. I think he's right—they are fascinating. How did anyone manage to come up with something like that? They didn't even consider balance or harmony with anything around it. *To hell with environmental aesthetics!* It's like a thumbed nose at the purists."

We got out of the car and took the elevator. As we got off on the third floor, an incredibly realistic ship's horn boomed out of nowhere. It seemed to reverberate to the depths of my stomach.

"Whoa! What the . . . So it is a ship inside as well. Pretty elaborate don't you think? Right down to the foghorn. Should we throw streamers from the windows, do you think? Don't you like this place?"

"I guess I'd call it vulgar."

"It's not vulgar. A bit childish, that's all."

"I feel like they're making fun of us."

"The foghorn?"

"They're taking the piss."

"Of course they're taking the piss. That's why it's fun. I bet they'll sound a gong or something next . . ." I sighed. "You prefer the usual place, then."

"Yes. I can relax in a place like that. You know—somewhere normal."

"You know that place may not look like a love hotel, but it's still just a pay-by-the-hour motel for lovers."

"Yes, but it's more tasteful than this place."

"Okay, I get it. But we're here now, so could you just put up with it this one time?"

It wasn't only that our tastes were different, it was that *something* just didn't mesh with us. That *something* was already uncomfortable for me, but I suspected that it was already grating on the man far more, and only likely to get worse. I didn't particularly care whether we visited a wild, eccentric building every time we met, nor was I totally entranced by some ship's horn. But it didn't matter what kind of setting we were in, we still had nothing to talk about. Out of simple curiosity, I had proposed that we board a luxury ocean liner. No, that's not quite it. I'd wanted to bug him, to tease that *something* different in this man. I knew he hated anything trashy. In the neighborhood of the hotel that he always patronized was another hotel done up to look like the kind of fairy-tale castle that Snow White might have lived in. Every time we drove past it, he would almost spit on it in contempt.

A cruise-ship love hotel far surpasses a Snow White castle love hotel in bad taste. At least a castle can be considered a structure normally built on land for people to inhabit. For an ocean liner, even to be on dry land is bizarre enough. For the kind of man who disliked anything trashy, the utter grotesqueness of this place was probably like the worst kind of horror movie. Snow White's castle simply provoked disgust; a giant passenger ship could never get away with mere disgust.

"Do you think that horn is set up to go off whenever someone steps out of the elevator?" I asked.

I could see that our *something different* was fast approaching *irreconcilable differences*, but sex still came naturally. Somehow there was no disconnect there—our bodies seemed to fit better than ever. We were able to devote our minds completely to what was happening inside our bodies. Each of us connected with the other solely for our own benefit, but we were still somehow able to share pleasure.

By now, I'd completely given up expecting any kind of verbal communication, and as my flesh began to fit with the flesh of this other being, I dropped any pretense of "sexual communication" either. I just wanted to get laid. The interval between the moment we met and the moment we finally had sex had become interminable. However, when that moment finally came, the sex was neither incredibly passionate nor were we into anything particularly unusual or kinky. To tell the truth, the sex we had was pretty much the same as the sexual activity an average forty-something man and woman might have in their marriage. Since there was hardly any intercourse with this man in the verbal world, our sexual intercourse took place in a kind of vacuum cut off from any emotional or spiritual curiosity about each other. And so I had come to think of the man as nothing more than a sex object. I ignored everything outside of his sexuality. I wondered if he'd ever rebel against that.

The ship's horn sounded again in the distance.

"Look—I can't be a frog. I've got a belly button." This was one of his rare jokes.

"That really did piss you off, didn't it, when I called you a frog," I grinned.

"Hey, did you hear those two sitting next to us that time say what a great couple we made?" he suddenly asked.

"I know. They were really annoying. We'd all introduced ourselves when we first sat down, so they already knew we weren't together. They were trying to catch us out or something. There were a lot of married couples there that day . . ."

"When she said that, I thought how great it would be to be married to you."

"You're too easily influenced by the power of suggestion."

"I'd been imagining what it'd be like to get rid of my wife and find someone younger and cuter."

"I hate the kind of man who casually tosses out lines about trading in his old wife for a new model. I always think if you really can't stand your wife, at least have the grace to divorce her first before you start going on about things like that. Guys who make macho pronouncements like that are usually the ones who don't have the balls to follow up."

"So what about your marriage?"

52

"I plan for us to grow contentedly old together."

"So you're just trailing along together."

"Trailing?"

"You're not?"

"What do you mean by *trailing*?"

"Does your husband write poetry too?"

"No."

"So his *jungle* is different from yours?"

Throughout the ensuing conversation, each time this man used the word *jungle* instead of *genre*, my heart started pounding. I'm sure he'd just misheard the term somewhere, but I hesitated to correct him for fear of offending him. It would have been easier to tell him if it were a Japanese word, but being an imported term, it was all the more difficult. Even though I had heard it and used it in Japanese, I really couldn't know for sure in what context or with what significance a French person would originally have used the term *genre*. Therefore, I wasn't really in a position to criticize someone else. Still a *genre* was pretty far from a *jungle*. I became totally distracted wondering how I could possibly get him to catch on to the fact that *jungle* was the wrong word.

However, the real issue here was not the mistaking of one term for another. What had truly depressed me was his casual dismissal of someone's marriage as "trailing along." I'd been stunned by his comment.

I was lost in a jungle of words.

"ASA 400 is more sensitive," he was saying.

"ASA 400?"

"It's the number that signifies the sensitivity of camera film. It means the sensitivity is good," he explained, like an adult teaching a child. It occurred to me that he might actually enjoy teaching and explaining things to people, but that he'd been holding back up till now.

"You know how you said that time that I ought to split up with my wife before I started talking about getting remarried? Well, my wife's always said that if I find someone else and want to get married that she'll gladly divorce me right away."

"Oh, really? I'm sure she only says that because she believes it'll never happen. Why don't you try it out?"

"I think my wife is very open about these things."

"So, go ahead and test her. But I know you'd never dare."

"Yeah, if I was thinking about getting married again I'd probably have to get divorced first."

"Well it'd certainly be less complicated. Anyway, why on earth do you want to marry someone young? Do you think she'll obey your every command? Or that every time you say jump, she'll jump? Do you think if you marry someone twenty years younger you can be like some kind of father figure to her, teaching her everything she needs to know?"

"Yeah, that's part of it. I think it's really cute when girls are young and naïve."

"I get it. Right, well next month I'm going abroad."

"For a vacation?"

"No I think I'll stay there some time. Maybe six months, maybe a year."

"What for?"

"Hmm. Perhaps I've decided it's time to get away from such a shitty guy," I said, then added: "Of course, that was a joke."

"So I'll be back to using my car for getting to work."

"It'll be peaceful for you again," I smiled.

"Don't make me use it just for commuting," he said brusquely.

I realized that his schedule was about to be disrupted. It was kind of fun for me to imagine.

The passenger seat of his car was taken up by a large brown paper parcel. Several sheets of photocopied paper were spilling from it all over the seat and floor. He deftly gathered them up and threw them onto the back seat.

"This is a load of bullshit," he said contemptuously.

I was amazed to hear him initiate a conversation.

"It's free to go to a public elementary or middle school, right? You have to have loads of money to bother sending your kid to one of those faraway, expensive private schools. If you can't afford it then you send your kid to the local public school. But now the private schools are asking for more subsidies from the government. It's not fair. Private schools are supposed to be financed by money from the kids' parents, so why can't they raise the fees? If it's too expensive for the parents then they can send their kids elsewhere. But at my place they're making a huge fuss over getting these subsidies."

"Aha. So you're a schoolteacher."

"No, I'm not."

"Then a janitor, perhaps?"

"Don't be ridiculous. Although I am on the staff. At any rate, they're always ranting on and on about unreasonable stuff."

"If you want a certain kind of education then you have to pay for it. If you don't want to pay then just send your kids to a regular place."

"Right!" he said, his face reddening with self-righteousness.

"But the parents aren't very likely to join you in your fight. They're going to support the subsidies. It doesn't matter who they are, parents use any means possible to try to get their child ahead. As for you, no matter how righteously angry you are, you are being paid a salary by that same school, so you're not in much of a position to oppose requests for government subsidies. What are those papers?"

The great friend of justice looked embarrassed and dropped his voice.

"It's a petition from my school asking the government for subsidies."

"You've collected that many signatures?" I asked, glancing at the back seat.

"I'm thinking of getting my wife to take it to her office, and asking our relatives to help out too."

"You're really being very cooperative," I said in amazement

"Well, I'm just a lowly employee," he said self-deprecatingly.

I couldn't believe the depth of personal humiliation he was putting himself through, especially considering his previous outburst. Still, I guessed that this emphatic indignation was partly intended as some sort of display for my benefit. He'd evidently agreed to collect more than his allotted share of signatures. This had made him all the angrier.

"I'm hoping to quit by the time I'm forty-five," he told me.

"And what do you plan to do after you quit?"

"I'd like to run my own business."

"Well that's easy to *say*. And by business you mean . . . ?"

"I guess it'll be hard."

"You can only give it a try."

"Yeah, there are many *jungles* of business."

"What? . . . Oh, yes I suppose there are . . ."

"At any rate the topics discussed in schools are very limited. It's a very insular community."

"If you hate it then you really ought to quit. There's no doubt about it. But isn't it a relatively easy job? Didn't you say you switched jobs to get more summer vacation?"

"It's certainly easy. Much easier than writing poetry, anyway."

"I told you I only used to write poetry when I was young."

"Well, you got published and everything."

"That's ancient history. And anyway, why don't you ask me for my signature on the petition?"

"I've got no reason to ask you."

"It's a hard life, being a lowly employee," I jibed with a smile.

"I don't know much about your field, but I suppose you have to make compromises to suit your publishers," he said with the air of a counterattack. "And well, you can't always afford to just do your own thing."

He wasn't exactly eloquent in his counterattack but he managed to make his meaning clear. He had experienced all the negative aspects of being a "lowly employee"—humiliation, anger, frustration, and finally, surrender. He was trying to say that, albeit in some other form, as I too earned my daily bread, I ought to have experienced all the same things. *You may be a disreputable hack, or a lone wolf or something, you may be able to spout clever words, but that's not enough to succeed. You must be brownnosing someone, doing something dirty.* It was a sneaky accusation.

"No, I get away with all kinds of bad stuff," I laughed.

"I don't believe you."

"I don't care what you think."

It hadn't been an obvious attack. It felt more like a spiteful attempt on his part to prove that I had something inside of me that was somehow similar to himself and his humiliating foolishness over the petition. It all made me feel as if we were on opposing sides. I could feel his hostility towards me. It might already be full-out war.

"So how do you feel about going on an overnight trip next Saturday?" I asked.

"Sounds great!" he responded, with his usual beaming smile.

6

We arrived after six, and were asked to head straight to the restaurant after taking our bags up to our room. Dinner was to be served at six thirty. The hotel was up in the mountains, on a kind of plateau that sloped gently upwards like the lid of a cooking pot. The squat, two-story building seemed to crouch there in the middle.

The hotel restaurant was bustling like a department store and packed with families eating dinner. The atmosphere was more like a hostel than a proper hotel. The tables were numbered according to room, and we found our meal already set out for us. There were thin slices of pork with spaghetti. The pork fillet had gone cold and the fat had turned to white wax. The ketchup-covered spaghetti looked as though it had been painted with an anemic shade of red paint, which had now begun to peel. It had clearly been stir-fried and the oil had begun to congeal so that the whole thing was stuck together in one big clump. I drank my beer and thought about eating, but I had no appetite for waxy pork and ketchup-painted noodles. I decided to try some of the other dishes on the table. I shoveled in some of the julienned cucumber and jellyfish in vinegar. The jellyfish crunched unpleasantly. I succeeded in cutting off a mouthful from a grilled fillet of fish that looked disturbingly like the plastic samples displayed in restaurant windows. It was incredibly salty and I swallowed it down as quickly as I could. Removing the lid from the plastic soup bowl, I found a thin, watery miso soup containing just a few meager shreds of wakame seaweed that had sunk to the bottom. And true to the tone of the meal so far, it was stone cold. There was an assortment of other side dishes: little bowls of edamame or tiny fish; a mysterious brown gelatinous substance on a long narrow plate; a crock pot of boiled mixed vegetables. Unfortunately, everything had been prepared so far in advance and left standing on the table for so long they were no longer chilled, but spoiling in the muggy air. The flavors were so bland they couldn't be labeled either delicious or disgusting.

I looked up. "I think I saw a Chinese restaurant on the other side of the highway not far back."

"Huh?" He looked at me in confusion. The waxy pork and congealed spaghetti had completely disappeared from the plate in front of him.

I abandoned my dream of escaping to the Chinese restaurant.

The lobby had a vaulted ceiling and a spiral staircase up to the second floor. As we climbed up to our room, we had a grand view of the huge, overly elaborate chandelier.

"I don't think there's a bar in this hotel," I remarked.

"They have everything you need here," he replied, opening the minifridge. The room had two beds, a love-seat-sized sofa, and a small table. I sat beside him on the love seat and downed a miniature of whiskey with a dash of water.

"So how are you feeling?" I asked in a cheery tone, attempting to improve the mood.

"We're really doing it—spending the night together. Not like that other time, when I had to drive around the whole night," he said.

This was a direct dig at me. We had made vague plans to spend the night once before, but I'd caught a bad cold and had to cancel. He had prepared a scheme in advance to explain to his wife why he had to be away for a night. Then, when my sudden cancellation made it impossible for him to go home that night, he apparently spent the night in his car. Now he was bringing it up again. He drank a shot of extremely watered-down whiskey. The room felt cramped.

"I booked on less than a week's notice, so this was all I could get," he explained.

"Don't you want another drink?"

"One's my limit."

"Well, then, let's talk about something interesting."

"Are you really going abroad next month?"

"I certainly am. I've already bought my plane ticket."

"So you're really going, then."

"Yes, I am."

"Wow. You really do live the good life."

"So, you want to go to bed?"

"But it's not even nine yet."

"That's what we came for, isn't it?"

"Yeah, I suppose . . . So where exactly are you going? France? America?"

"It's a secret. If I tell you, you'll only follow me there," I said with a grin.

The man didn't smile. His face was as expressionless as ever.

It could have been peace of mind, the knowledge that this time he didn't have to hurry home afterwards, but all his movements seemed slow and methodical—the manner in which he poured hot water from the thermos pot into his teacup and drank it, the way he took off his clothes seemed habitual, even mundane. It felt as if he was going through his usual routine without even acknowledging my presence. He had become totally aloof. There was no feeling whatsoever of unity between us. It was as if he had retreated into his own little cocoon, and was protected from any deviation from the norm—or in other words, me.

He had brought with him a well-used, oversized vinyl shoulder bag which he now opened to take out what appeared to be a bag of toiletries. At the same time, he placed a camera and several rolls of films on the table. These reeked of the kind of disguise put together by a man cheating on his wife for a night. Obviously, he wasn't going to be taking pictures of me with that camera.

"That's a nice bag," he remarked, picking up my own shoulder bag from the table.

My bag was feminine and burgundy-colored. It was a simple bag, just a little larger than the one I usually used for my makeup.

"Hey, you could easily fit a magazine or a book in here too. It's just the right size for a man," he said, practically caressing it.

"You want it?"

"Yeah."

"Well, I need it for the rest of this trip, but I'll give it to you next time I see you. I really liked it when I bought it but I'm not that keen on it anymore."

"But it looks expensive. Are you sure?"

"I said you could have it, so it's yours."

Then the two of us squeezed side by side into one of the twin beds and proceeded to have sex. It had become mechanical. The man was confident of my body's responses. He was so sure that sex with me was going to feel good for him that he was on autopilot.

As soon as we'd finished I headed to the sofa to drink another watered-down whiskey.

"Last week I went fishing with a group from work. I went for a walk on the beach that night with one of the older guys. I suddenly said how I wished I was with my lover on such a starry night," the man said.

"What did you say?"

"I said I wanted to be with my lover under those stars."

"Well, that's a total cliché."

"It just slipped out. You know—the word *lover*."

"That's what I'm saying. Everyone says that sort of thing when they're on a beach looking at the stars."

"It just came out. *With my lover . . .*"

Apparently, he believed that he had just confessed his love for me through this supposedly true story. How he had accidentally blurted out to some elderly colleague on a beach under a starry sky that he wanted to be there with his lover. I guess that lover was supposed to be me. The man had used his colleague to confess and simultaneously define himself as someone who had a lover. It could safely be assumed, however, that the old man who had heard the "confession" had merely thought he was hearing a cli-chéd generalization.

"I just came right out with it!" The man kept repeating this in a sort of personal euphoria.

So, to summarize, he had intended to say to his colleague, *I have a lover. I want to be with this lover here on this starry beach, and I really shouldn't have to be stuck here with an old fart like you, instead.* Or perhaps, more to the point, he wanted to show off to me that he had said it. Instead of telling me straight out that one beautiful starry night on the beach he'd wished we'd been together, he'd gone the roundabout route of the story about the elderly colleague. Direct versus indirect speech. I didn't believe this indirect speech was from any kind of shyness—I found it rather arrogant. He was the one who had decided I was his lover. It didn't matter what I thought or felt about it—he just wanted to believe that he had a lover. Whatever the case, the story of the hypothetical lover sounds ridiculous to the person who's been cast in the role of "The Lover." And talking about an imaginary lover made him sound like some pathetic guy trying to sound popular. Pitiful.

"I guess this isn't something you say in front of your wife?" I asked.

"To tell the truth, sometimes over dinner, right when I'm telling her how good the meal is, sometimes I almost want to fess up," he replied.

His use of the phrase *fess up* made me feel nauseous. I knew it was a really popular phrase with kids these days, but hearing it come from this guy's mouth, it came out like some kind of alien language. He was like some sort of creature that had covered itself from head to toe with a suit of armor, but despite all the armor plating, he was still as slippery and slimy as a tadpole.

"If I'm not careful, it'll all just come spewing out," the tadpole elaborated.

I detected on my armor-plated tadpole something like the stench of a sewer, like the reek of stagnant, mosquito-infested water, like the stink of unchanged water in a fish tank, the way greenish-black water smells. I desperately needed to change the subject.

"Did you ever go back to those seminars?" I asked.

"No, it was just that one time."

"I heard they were once a month. I guess it doesn't matter whether you're serious about learning or not. Those speakers are really interesting."

The municipal government would dispatch an expert on local history to the cultural center, right next to that archaeological dig site, to give a monthly lecture on the history of the local area—those rolling hills and valleys that had offered up so many relics of the past. The time we attended, right after the local history expert finished, a teacher from a private high school in P——yato gave a lecture on ancient Korean culture and its effect on Japan. Then he followed up his talk with a simple class in basic Korean. I'd met the man at lunch between the lecture and the language workshop.

"So did you practice any Korean after that?" I asked.

"Yeah, a colleague of mine had asked me to go with him that time and had to drop out at the last minute, but he was really keen and had loaned me a language-learning tape. I don't really have much interest or talent for learning, though. I learned how to say *hello, good-bye, thank you*, and that's about it."

"I was curious so I just went that time. Especially as you can't get the textbook or the tape at an ordinary bookstore. But just a minute—I remember as you were leaving you said 'good-bye' to the teacher in Korean and you were all smiles. The other students looked impressed too. I think that day you were the only one who got out a single word of Korean—*hello, good-bye, thank you* or whatever. Must have been because you'd studied before the class, that's why it came out so naturally. You looked so proud."

"I looked proud, did I?" he mused, with evident pride.

"It's funny about foreign languages. Anyone who can speak even a few words looks impressive to those who don't speak it at all."

"I'll ask my colleague where he bought the tape, if you like."

"Thanks, but I've already got it."

I lay there in the dark with my eyes wide open, not bothering to make any more conversation. After a while, I heard the man's breathing change. It felt strange to have another human being lying right next to me. A complete stranger was lying there like a log, totally vulnerable. He was like a foreign object to me. I felt more fellowship when my dog was sleeping in my room. The presence of this sleeping man only gave me the sense that some kind of foreign substance had penetrated the space around me.

Unlike a toothache, the feeling of sexual satisfaction doesn't continue indefinitely, and I already felt so removed from it, it could have happened in the distant past. If you're someone who believes that human sexual satisfaction is inexorably linked with spiritual rapport, in other words with love, then I guess you'd think I have a heart of stone. But I contend that it's a lie that's been perpetuated by some textbook theory of human life and relationships, to claim that female sexual fulfillment is only completed by loving and being loved, and settling comfortably into the crook of a man's arm for a tranquil night's sleep.

He had sought an affair with a married woman; for me the circumstances were irrelevant—I was just fucking a man. The man got excited the first time we had sex because it was an extremely unusual experience for him. However, because he believed in the myth that to have sex with a woman other than his wife must be either an affair or prostitution, he was uncomfortable with my own desire simply to have sex. He couldn't believe it possible that a woman might be after nothing more than sexual gratification from a man. He believed that, while a man is able to require just a specific part of a woman, in contrast a woman always desires the whole of a man. Yet he didn't have it in him to participate fully in the drama of a real love affair.

"Don't you know the name of the place you're inside of?" I had once asked him during sex. He'd been unable to bring himself to say it. When I urged him to "say it together with me," counted to three and said it loudly, he'd kept his mouth firmly shut.

"For women I think it's all about atmosphere," he would say.
"That's just what you think. Actually we can do it anytime, anywhere," I told him.

For all that, for the man's sake, I still said "I love you" before sex. This was not a concession on my part, letting him believe we were having a romantic affair. It was my role reversal of the woman who, seeking reassurance before sleeping with a man, asks, "Do you love me?" to which the man responds, "Of course I love you." It gave me a sense of power.

It had struck me that the very fact that all I wanted was sex could, in itself, be considered a form of aggression towards the man. Unfortunately, whenever I thought like this, it seemed to give rise to an even stronger desire to be aggressive. *All I want from you is sex, instant gratification—now!*

The man began to snore like a runner gasping for breath.

I figured that after we left this hotel I would probably never see him again. I'd been bored by the lack of verbal communication and had desired sex for communication, but I'd gotten bored of that too, and now there was nothing left to be desired from him.

He had once said to me, "I expect your husband caresses you more tenderly than I do. I'm sure he satisfies you much better sexually."

I knew what response would have made him happy. He wanted to hear that my husband failed to satisfy me sexually and so I had turned to him as a sexual outlet, and had found that he could satisfy all my desires. Or alternatively, that I had an extremely high sex drive and that my husband wasn't man enough to satisfy me, and so I had turned to this man and now I was fulfilled. Either way, he was eager to have his own role acknowledged, and to be compared favorably. I knew what he was after, but I didn't bite. I couldn't compare my whole relationship with my husband to a quick-fix genital coupling. I guess if I'd told him my husband was impotent, he'd have been ecstatic. It was likely that he had no clue as to why I had repeatedly slept with him. If it wasn't from love, and it wasn't from unhappiness in my marriage, then what on earth was it?

"For fun? Curiosity? It's definitely not my looks because I've never been lucky with women."

What could I say to make him feel better? In the first place, sex is not everything. Secondly, I'm no Lady Chatterley. If I wasn't satisfied by my husband, I would have chosen someone who was more of a man—someone like Lady Chatterley's lover, to be exact.

He was still gasping loudly. I tugged at the blanket that covered his body. He was wearing a *yukata* cotton kimono several sizes too small, which had ridden up over the lower half of his body. His shriveled penis lay exposed and defenseless. The moment I touched it, the snoring stopped and he instinctively braced himself. Then he saw me, and gave a little smile of approval, the kind of gesture you would give to a lover. In response, I suddenly felt belligerent. My sexual desire for this man was purely aggressive. What kind of loser was it who spread that groundless rumor that women were sexually passive? The darkness outside was slowly turning to morning—a pale light was beginning to filter through the transparent material of the cheap curtains.

It was still only eight thirty by the time we'd eaten breakfast, but he suggested we get going. He explained that if it got too late, everyone would be leaving and the roads would be crowded.

"It'll be a pain if we get stuck in traffic like yesterday."

"If we leave this early we'll be home really quickly. It won't even be noon."

"I told my wife I'd be back in the morning."

"Oh, you did, did you?"

The winding mountain roads, the national highways and the expressway all seemed like different roads from the previous day. There was hardly a car to be seen on any of them at first. Even the scenery looked different. Ordinarily people thought of Sunday as a time to go on a day trip. Then, by the evening, the roads would be jammed with cars heading home. The only people heading towards the city early Sunday morning were couples who had gotten into their cars the previous day and headed for the mountains for the sole purpose of having sex.

"That knife and fork symbol is for a roadside restaurant, right? Could we stop there?" I asked.

There were quite a lot of people at this large rest stop. They were clearly setting out on their day trips.

"Oh, look what they have here. Rooms for long-distance truck drivers to take a nap. I guess you can rent by the hour. So they had places like that . . ." said the man, as he hurried back to the car with his can of soda.

He was looking at a bleak building that reminded me of a hospital ward. He was harping on once again about the night when I'd begged off because I had a fever. He never actually said something like, "That night I was so miserable," or "I felt so lonely." He was airing his grievances by insinuation. And this was already the second time he'd done it.

"So next time, you can stay there. Look, did you really not stop anywhere that night?"

"Hey, it's fine."

"If that's the case, either air your grievances out in the open, or say nothing at all."

"I'm really not bothered about it."

"So if you're not bothered about it, shut up. If it was me, I wouldn't go on about it. Even if I'd slept on a bench at the train station. Let's go, shall we?"

I knew that he was beginning to get mad with me. His feeling of anger was general and very vague, and the only way he'd found to express it was through retaliation for something that had been an unpleasant experience for him like the night spent in his car. The undefined anger that was beginning to consume him stemmed, in all probability, from being used for sex. If I had been passive in the relationship, he would have been able to enjoy the pursuit of a woman's body. But he hadn't been able to get that with me, there had been no thrill of the hunt, and he had no idea how to understand the situation. It would have been far easier to deal with romantic feelings, but there were none in this case. It wasn't even one of those traditional patron/bar hostess types of relationship, involving some measure of financial support. No, there was really no way for him to come to terms with our relationship.

"I need to use the facilities," he announced.

"You mean the bathroom?"

"Please wait for me in the car," he said, handing me the keys.

This man hadn't been able to bring himself to say the words *bathroom* or *toilet*. It occurred to me that he'd probably never spoken the words in his life.

"Let's go and fill up," he said when he came back from the toilet.

"So did you have a good piss?"

He ignored me and pulled up at the pump.

After we left the gas station, neither of us spoke. We drove along the deserted roads and eventually reached the familiar hill country. It was still only just after eleven, bright and sunny—the kind of day where you could see things too clearly. I took off my sunglasses and looked the man in the eyes.

"Thank you."

"Nice sunglasses."

"You're not getting these as well."

"They don't look as if they were made in Japan."

"You know, I don't know where they were made. I just bought them to protect my eyes. Could you let me out at T—— station?"

"I'll drive you home if you want, let you out at the usual place."

"No, T—— station will be fine. I've got some shopping to do."

"Are you really going abroad?"

"Yes, I'm really going abroad. Ah, that reminds me. I haven't given you my half of the hotel bill yet."

"It's okay."

"We'll split it. If you're always trying to be nice you'll never make it in your own business."

"So you can make that much money out of writing poems?"

"Poetry is not a way of making money. And I've already told you, my days as a poet are over. Now I just live day to day."

I made my way into the station coffee shop, a little unsteady on my feet from lack of sleep, and drank two cups of coffee in an attempt to wake myself up. I completely forgot about the man. All I felt was a sensation of freedom, a release from the confined space of his car and from him.

7

My friend Kumiko had seen me in the cream-colored car with the man and asked to be introduced. Kumiko was single and lived alone in a rented apartment in my neighborhood. Ever since graduating from university she'd lived away from her parents and supported herself. I told Kumiko that the man wasn't single, but she laughed and said that wasn't her reason for meeting him. I told her how annoying it was that he disliked *enka* songs and was always singing traditional folk songs, and she thought that was cute. She said she always hated it when middle aged men got all self-absorbed singing *enka*. Kumiko was thirty years old.

I was going abroad, so I wasn't going to be able to observe first-hand how Kumiko got along with the man.

"I'll write and keep you up to date," she promised.

When he called, I told him about Kumiko, explained I'd given her the burgundy shoulder bag to pass along to him, and gave him her phone number. I hadn't seen him since our overnight trip.

I left without seeing Kumiko either. She kept her promise and wrote with a passion. I always looked forward to her letters, and used them as inspiration to dream up even more tales about the characters involved.

My intuition told me that Kumiko and the man would have a lot more in common than their dislike of *enka* music. He'd told me that he hated women wearing makeup. "My wife never wears any," he had proudly informed me. I joked that women were such ugly beings that a bit of makeup was essential, but I didn't raise any serious objections to his preferences. Kumiko always had that freshly-scrubbed look, as if she never used anything on her face but soap. This didn't come off as lazy—it suited her perfectly. She gave off a wholesome image, like a fresh-faced schoolboy.

Her first letter contained astonishing news. It turned out she'd visited the man's home and eaten dinner with him and his wife. She was already on first-name terms with both *Katsumi* and his wife *Ayako*. Despite our separation in time and place, her letters bridged the gap between us so well I felt as though I were there.

So did you give him the bag? I scribbled on the back of a picture postcard, along with my new address. She responded that as soon as she'd handed it to him he'd stuck it in the trunk of his car, and that she hadn't seen it since.

Back when he asked for the bag, I'd said, "Are you really going to use it? If I see some other woman using it on the train or around the station, I'll be really mad. So make sure to use it yourself, okay?" I'd been unusually particular about my instructions. So what had become of that bag?

I'd open my eyes around dawn, and try to go back to sleep, but the more I thought about sleeping, the more impossible it was. At times like that, I always seemed to get to thinking about the whereabouts of that burgundy-colored bag. I had hardly used it, so it could easily be taken for a brand-new bag. Had he given it as a present to his wife? I'd already suspected he might from the moment he'd started stroking and fawning over it. In spite of its very simple design, anyone would recognize at a glance that it was a woman's bag. I was sure he wasn't taking it to work. That bag had ended up a gift from husband to wife. I'd already been convinced of that when I gave it to him. That was why I had decided so suddenly to let him have it—I was interested in what would become of my bag. Or to be honest, I was interested in the man's poverty; or rather, shaming him for this feigned poverty. This wasn't somebody who couldn't afford to buy a bag. Here was a man who vacationed abroad with his wife in summer. But his look had betrayed that he might consider another woman's bag an appropriate gift for that same wife.

Kumiko reported that Ayako didn't appear to have the bag. If it wasn't his wife, had he given it away to some young thing? I found I was hanging on the next letter from Kumiko.

The fantasies I had after reading her stories helped me to deal with my urge to be cruel to the man, even though I was far away. Of course, these cruel desires could never be acted upon anywhere but in my own fantasies. But her letters helped me work through my urges, including a nagging thirst for revenge, even though he'd done nothing to me to warrant any kind of revenge. What was it? There was no score to settle. I guess I just wanted to torment him.

I knew, however, that he was simply too wholesome and cheerful to be affected by my sick brand of cruelty, so it had to stay in my fantasies; otherwise I would drive myself insane. I could bet my life that no idea that I could come up with, however sick, would ever penetrate this man's defenses. It would just be shadow-boxing, and I knew it.

Kumiko wrote that she and Ayako so closely resembled each other it was unnerving:

> Coming home to your own house, opening the door to your own room, sitting at your own desk and picking up a book or something, you might catch sight of your own back and almost fall off your chair. Walking along an empty road, you could meet yourself coming from the opposite direction and jump out of your skin. They say that if you ever meet yourself this way in real life, this means you're about to die.

Kumiko said she remembered having read all this somewhere, and consequently, when she'd first met Ayako she'd been terrified. But then she'd realized that in the scary story she'd read, it was always your own self that you met, your own self that you caught sight of; it was never someone who looked just like you. Then Kumiko relaxed and thought of Ayako simply as someone who resembled herself.

Ayako had the same boyish short haircut, and, like Kumiko, never wore makeup.

I'd asked the man, "So you're saying that you like a woman who smells of soap?"

"Yes, I like a woman who smells pure and clean, as if she's just taken a bath."

"You've been taken in by a myth. Women don't smell of soap. Do you think that soap is what 'clean' smells like? Women can't remove their odor simply by washing with soap."

That was all I said. Just like cheese, some people find the way a woman smells offensive, but there are others who find it one of the most delightful scents they've ever savored. To tell the truth, I hadn't been thinking of anything particular when I began talking of a woman's odor, but by the time this conversation took place, I already knew that this man always agreed with popular opinion, so there was no point in saying any more.

Whenever Ayako had a guest over she would pour tea, then sit and crochet. Kumiko was amazed, as this was her habit too. There were white lace doilies and mats all over Ayako's home; on top of the TV, under the telephone, on the tea cabinet, the back of an armchair, and as a dining-table centerpiece. This also amazed Kumiko. There were white lace doilies all over her own home. And whenever she and Ayako were seated symmetrically on either side of Katsumi, she'd always recall the story of the person who died after meeting himself.

I never got tired of hearing this kind of information from Kumiko.

It took Ayako two hours every day to commute from the K—— apartment complex to her job in M—— city. Neither Kumiko nor the man needed to commute all the way into the city. Kumiko took a short bus ride to the pharmaceutical company in Y—— town where she worked, and the man's office was right on the edge of Y——. Just like the man, Kumiko was very familiar with the hill country and the geography of the area. She had once taken me to a Noh and Kyogen performance at the Y—— municipal theater. In fact, Kumiko never passed up this kind of free program, always applying early for tickets, distributed on a first-come first-served basis.

I went to the K—— Gakuin school bazaar with Ayako, wrote Kumiko. There was Ayako's name again! In fact, these days she seemed to write about no one else. I was dying to know what had become of the man. It had only been a month since I left, but already Kumiko and Ayako seemed joined at the hip.

Obviously, I wasn't going to be sending the man any postcards. I hadn't written much to Kumiko either for that matter. But I knew Kumiko loved writing letters. She was always about to write to somebody . . .

On Sunday we drove up to Lake S——, on the border with the next prefecture. Ayako had something or other come up at the last minute, so it was just Katsumi and me. It was Ayako who had invited me to join them, so it was kind of weird to end up going there just with Katsumi. The maples were a stunning shade of red. It was a Sunday but the roads were empty and we sped along. We drove for so long through tunnels of crimson leaves that you started to get the eerie feeling that beyond the trees, the water of the lake itself must be bright red too. So like a little kid, I started to sing to take my mind off it. Katsumi has quite a good voice. We sang together—that song you really hate—Song of the Seasons. It seems Katsumi and I have exactly the same taste in music. And Ayako too, of course. Ayako is a member of the chorus club at her company. And just like me, she's a big fan of your number-one pet peeve—organic foods. We really are alike, you know. You know if you met her, you'd be struck speechless by how alike we are. When Ayako and I are walking together, people turn and stare, so it seems everyone thinks we look alike. The only major difference between us is that Ayako is very shy. She speaks very softly too.

On the way back from Lake S——, Katsumi took me to a very unusual place, even though it was a bit out of the way. Apparently, they had taken a historic family dwelling, complete with its massive triangular thatched roof, straight out of that World Heritage village in Gifu Prefecture—Shirakawa—and moved it here to be used as a restaurant. It even had a little river running through the house itself. Well, not a real river, but a twenty-inch-wide manmade stream with the water running through fairly quickly. Your order would be sent floating down the stream to your table and there was some kind of device to make it stop by the right table. Rainbow and Yamane trout arrived on little boats, and we grilled them on an irori hearth in our private dining room. I was really impressed that Katsumi had discovered such an interesting place in the middle of nowhere.

Ayako likes to stay at home on Sundays to get the house straightened up, and she doesn't really like going for drives anyway. She says she appreciates my spending time with Katsumi. Ayako is always saying to Katsumi how glad she is that he has such great company. Katsumi grins when Ayako says this. Even the drive up to Lake S—— was Ayako's idea. I agreed to go if Ayako went with us, and she promised to come, but in the end she said she couldn't make it. With Ayako, you know, we're both women, we're completely alike, so I feel comfortable around her. I still enjoy it when it's just Katsumi and me, but I can't completely relax and it ends up being exhausting. Katsumi is quite a gentleman, don't you think? Still, he doesn't talk about you when we're around Ayako. Well, me neither. We really don't have anything to talk about when we're alone though, so naturally then the conversation turns to you. Well, to be exact, it's never Katsumi who starts the conversation. And whenever I mention you, he just laughs and says, "She called me a frog."

I've never wanted to get married. I think you already know that. And that's still how I feel. But it's not because I'm a lesbian or anything. I don't even feel that way about Ayako. It's going to sound weird, but the proof is that I've recently started to obsess more and more about having a baby. If you were here, you'd just come right out and say it like you always do—"Wow, looks like Kumiko's finally in heat." Even if I tell you that's not it, you'll still laugh at me. But, you know, I have actually been in love before.

So what do you do over there every day? Is your husband well? Could you at least write to me once? Are you that busy? Are you working? Have you at least come across any interesting books? Bring back a book that might sell. I'm sure translation work is boring unless the original's good. Find a good thriller or something. You know, Dick Francis or someone.

Katsumi invited me to go out for Chinese with him, and he took me to the seaside. After that, we went down to the harbor. I stood there staring at the sea and the boats. Suddenly he said, "It's getting too late to go home tonight." Did he say the same thing to you, Kyoko?

He said it again when we got in the car, "At this rate we won't be able to get home." What should I do? Please tell me, what kind of a person is Katsumi?

I couldn't help chuckling as I read Kumiko's letters. The thatched-roof restaurant, the Chinese restaurant near the harbor, Lake S——: these were all places I'd been with him. And here was the man, leading Kumiko around as if it were the first time he'd ever been there. Even the rainbow and *yamane* trout were the same. The only thing different was the pick-up line. I hadn't used that outdated phrase, "It's getting too late to go home tonight," like some kind of coy schoolgirl. And I'm sure Kumiko, unlike the man, had at least refused the first couple of times. Now everything was going his way. He'd gone on the offensive in pursuit of Kumiko, using the same methods as I had with him. I felt like cheering him on. I was sure Kumiko would love that "tasteful, not vulgar" love hotel. Kumiko also hated trashy stuff.

It was some time before another letter from Kumiko arrived. Well, by that I mean that there was a whole week before I got another one. She wrote how she'd invited the man to her apartment and cooked him pasta. She described the menu and included colorful sketches: tuna-and-anchovy spaghetti, a seafood salad, cheesecake, and coffee. Aha, that was the exact same thing I'd cooked for Kumiko the first time she came to my house. Kumiko had begged me for the recipe, so I was the one who had taught her how to make tuna-and-anchovy spaghetti.

But I was far more interested in the fact that, as Kumiko lived alone, the man would be able to go to her apartment instead of the tasteful love hotel.

In the next letter, Kumiko wrote that at Ayako's suggestion she had joined the Veggie Club. The Veggie Club was part of a movement to get people to buy natural, organic produce. I guessed the reason that Ayako didn't wear makeup was related to her food choices—she must like the all-natural look. Kumiko was also the all-natural type. She put nothing on her body that wasn't from nature. Her clothes were made from cotton, hemp, or wool; she refused to buy any man-made fibers such as nylon or polyester.

So now they had that in common, too.

Kumiko's address changed. It appeared she'd moved to K—— town, close to the K—— apartment complex. She wrote that this was in part for ease of contact with the Veggie Club, and partly so she could go jogging with Ayako. Not only had they started jogging together, but they were also responsible for dividing up and delivering the vegetables to the other Veggie Club members. Ayako also helped another all-natural group to sell pure loofah extract by introducing it to all the housewives in her apartment complex. It seemed Kumiko was assisting her.

I live alone so I can never get through a whole daikon radish. I always end up throwing half of it away, wrote Kumiko. *Every member receives so many vegetables. I don't know what to do with them all.*

What exactly is the definition of *natural*? Are there really any truly "natural" foodstuffs still in existence in this world? I wondered what exactly their rigorous standards might be.

Kumiko and Ayako's communication sounded intense. How was the man going to be able to carry out his assault on Kumiko, I wondered. Did he still drive around during his free time from four thirty to seven P.M.? Did Kumiko ever ride with him?

"It takes talent to make something this simple taste so bad. Even an amateur cook like me can make something that tastes better than this," I had said to the man over a bowl of spaghetti in a family restaurant. "You only have to use the same techniques as when you make soba or udon noodles."

He had sat there contentedly devouring the overcooked, soggy bowl of spaghetti. Then, as always, we went to a love hotel. However, this time not his beloved, tasteful hotel but a building done up outside to look exactly like a mosque. In the lobby there was a board featuring illuminated color photos of all the rooms. You chose the room that looked exciting to you, pressed its photo, and just like shaking out an *omikuji* fortune stick from a wooden box at a Buddhist temple or Shinto shrine, the key fell out into your hand. The hotel rooms were labeled A, B, and C. The letters corresponded to the price of the rooms, but I didn't notice at the time. My companion, the consumer of natural, organic produce, was so disgusted by the artificial trashiness of his surroundings that he just stood there morosely. In contrast, I, Ingester of Toxins Extraordinaire, felt like a little kid in a candy store. The vivid colors in the photos reminded me of the shiny pictures of food on the family-restaurant menu. Or pictures in a catalog. You pressed your fingertip against the picture you liked. Then you got something nice. The love hotel and restaurant both. I stood there drooling over all the pictures, wondering out loud which one would be the most entertaining. Mmm, the one with the bed shaped like a classic car, that'd be fun. Press the button and out pops the key.

On the way out, you paid at a window that looked exactly like the ticket booth at a movie theater. Next to it, and impossible to miss, was what looked like a department-store display window. It was a glass case with fluorescent lighting featuring rows of various-sized handbags. They were all imported brand-name bags, the kinds popular with young women. Next to each bag was a price tag, but instead of yen the currency was points. They ran from fifty to three hundred points. When we paid, we got a ticket worth one point. If you collected three hundred of these tickets, you could win a free bag. Three hundred times? In complete seriousness, the man picked up the ticket and tucked it into my pocket, saying, "Why don't you keep this?" I wondered if there really were people who, simply to obtain a Gucci handbag, collected three hundred of these one-point tickets with the love hotel's name clearly written and the manager's official stamp. I supposed there must be. One time, one point. Three hundred times, one handbag. I wondered how trashy Kumiko would find that.

Gradually, the edges around the separate personae of Kumiko and Ayako were blurring, and I was beginning to see them as one and the same person. This person was neither one hundred percent Kumiko nor one hundred percent Ayako. Kumiko and Ayako overlapped to make one persona, the shadow of a completely separate being. This shadowy human shape would overlap with Kumiko and Kumiko would disappear; it would overlap with Ayako and Ayako would disappear. This entity was both Kumiko and Ayako, yet at the same time, neither of them.

I even began to imagine that the man lived with this "being." Kumiko and Ayako were always together, after all.

Ayako speaks to Kumiko . . .

"Next Sunday is our company sports day, so I can't visit my mother like I usually do. Could you possibly go with Katsumi in my place?"

"Instead of you? For most things, sure, but not a visit to your mother."

"It'll be fine. My husband hates going to see my mother by himself. So please, Kumiko, would you?"

"It's *your* parents' home!"

"It'll be okay, as it's you."

"What do you mean, as it's me?"

"It'll be okay. It's only to drop off a couple of things."

In the end, Kumiko gets in Katsumi's car and goes to visit Ayako's mother. Or rather, I imagine she probably does.

Ayako always speaks in a soft voice, hardly more than a whisper. Kumiko has never once heard her shout, yell, or even laugh out loud. When Katsumi says something, Ayako replies, "Sounds great!" in a sickeningly sweet voice. Whenever Katsumi says he's going out, she always responds with, "Sounds great! See you later, then!" Apparently, she has never said, "No way!" or "Don't go."

I recalled how from time to time the man would unconsciously mimic the exact wording and tone of his wife's speech. Ayako always saw her husband off on a drive or an overnight trip by saying, "Sounds great! See you later, then!" and always welcomed him home with, "Did you have a good time? I'm really glad. The leaves must already have turned red. That's wonderful. I'm so glad you went right when you did."

"I've bought a cheesecake. Do you want to come over?" Kumiko would ask Ayako.

"Sounds great!" she'd say, and come running over to Kumiko's apartment in her wooden clogs.

Kyoko, I'm sure you've been imagining that Katsumi and I are more than just friends, but please don't jump to conclusions. I'm friends with both Katsumi and Ayako alike. Katsumi has none of that pushiness you get in so many men his age. He's totally safe, a perfect gentleman. He's completely fine with me getting close to Ayako. She knows that I live alone and really looks out for me. She'd never say it out loud, but I think Ayako worries that I must feel lonely all by myself. She was the one who suggested that Katsumi come over to my place to listen to records with me (that was the time I told you about when I cooked him spaghetti.) The Veggie Club, jogging together, that's all her idea. Actually all three of us go jogging together.

I see the three of them setting off running along the path through the center of K—— apartment complex, descending its gentle slope, then going up the wider, much steeper asphalt road. Before long, they come to an intersection with a small general store. Plenty of cars drive by, but there is hardly anyone else on foot. Under the bright rays of the sun, the asphalt shimmers white, as if covered with a paper lining. Some of the hills have not yet been completely deforested. The deciduous trees have mostly already turned brown, but here and there mixed in among them are some that are still green. The three figures keep running. The two women overlap from time to time and become one figure. The large man is sandwiched between the two of them. His heavy frame heaves up and down with his labored breathing, the flab on his back rolls in waves. The two petite women fall into exact step with each other, then separate again. Their identically-cut, short, straight hair swishes from side to side like needles hanging in a row. The women's breathing also becomes heavier. Sweat begins to appear on their foreheads, necks, shoulders, and breasts. Another downward slope. Another upward slope. The women's shoulders rise and fall in waves with their strained breathing.

"I'm struggling," pants Kumiko.

"Don't worry, just a little further," replies Ayako.

Ayako's pace never varies.

"We're almost there, right?" asks Kumiko.

"Don't talk," says Ayako.

"Where's Katsumi?" asks Kumiko.

Ayako doesn't respond. They're running along a wide, deserted road through one of the valleys. The large man has fallen behind the women and is practically walking. A water tower comes into sight. It's the one that serves the K—— apartment complex. Ayako turns the corner by the library. Kumiko follows. The man has caught up with Kumiko. For an instant, their eyes meet, and then they both look away. Kumiko speeds up to try to catch Ayako.

"Ayako, wait!"

Ayako was a middle-distance runner in high school, so her running style is different from mine. She's teaching me, and recently it's stopped getting so painful in the middle of a run. If I can push through the first burn, then somehow I seem to get in the zone after that. It's like some kind of drug. When I run, I forget that I'm running at all. With every single breath, I feel like I can run more and

more. At first, we just ran around the perimeter of the K—— apart-
ment complex, but lately we've made it as far as the B—— ruins.
The view around there is so beautiful that we almost find ourselves
running too far. The guard at the B——ruins has a dog. I think both
Ayako and Katsumi must dislike animals. This is a cute Shiba Inu
that has just about reached adulthood, but when I tried to stop to
visit with it, Ayako made me keep going. Katsumi doesn't go out
running with us any more. He only went with us twice. He doesn't
seem to be bothered about putting on weight. Next Saturday, he's
going to take me out for dinner for my birthday. I can't believe I'm
going to be thirty-one. Please come back soon.

I suddenly recalled the sexual desire I'd felt for this man. It seemed
that this was the only context I really remembered him in. At first,
in order to dress up the relationship a little I'd tried to add some
background color, using scenery or food. None of my words could
ever get a decent conversation going, so we'd always have to go
somewhere and always ended up having something to eat. To me,
that was the least common courtesy that I should show the man.

And then we'd gone on that overnight trip. I was so bored of him
that I'd wanted to have sex right away, but instead I'd said things
like, "Let's have some coffee," or "I'm hungry." But the man had
already abandoned all the rituals normally observed before sex.
Sex was all he was after. Although I felt the same way really, it still
annoyed me that he had changed. It was unpleasant for me to see
that this man had become so overly familiar with me.

On the way back from the trip he had said, "I really want to see
you one more time before you go abroad," which translated as "I
really want to fuck you one more time." I hadn't replied, which

translated as "No." I broke it off because he only wanted sex. I admit that I too was only interested in him for sex, but the difference was that I also made some effort to enjoy the scenery, chat, eat something delicious . . . I never stopped doing that. Nor did I overdo it. I did just about what was appropriate.

At first, the man found all these details interesting because it was a whole new experience to him, but as he got used to everything, he started to become neglectful. In the end, he went straight from getting me into his car to having sex. He really couldn't be bothered any more to spare the time, or even the cash, to drink a cup of coffee first. This was a man who had given up showing any courtesy, and had become completely boorish. I despised him for it.

I know, of course, that I'm contradicting myself. I hated dressing sex up to be something more than it was, yet at the same time I despised this man for reducing everything to sex.

From the beginning, the man had offered me nothing but his sexual desire. It was just that he never imagined that a woman could do the same thing. The object of my desire was the man's body (not the man himself) but the man believed that for me, i.e. the woman, that the object of my desire must be his body plus his personality in one neat package. When it came to sex with me, he must have felt as if his mind had been severed from his body. I completely ignored him as a person. If he'd asked me for money, I might have paid him. But as he was in fact only an amateur, for his sake I had controlled my aggressive sexuality, and added plenty of background color. Still in the end, the man was the one who had decided to skip the niceties and just get down to business.

The satisfaction of sexual desire is purely self-indulgent. Maybe even tyrannical. My desire for the man was fueled by a rage to attack. When a woman's sexuality ceases to be passive, it often turns into full-on aggression. The man was completely ignorant of this. It's possible within the sexual act for a man and woman to achieve pleasure entirely separately. The idea of synchronized pleasure is nothing but a concocted fantasy.

I know that some kind of deeper emotional connection with the man could have helped to calm my aggression. Instead, I had pounced on and tried to destroy the strength and wholesomeness of this ridiculous armor-plated tadpole. That was the base of my sexual desire for this man. He was ignorant of my aggression, and then I attacked him for that same ignorance.

"I really want to see you one more time before you go abroad." He was able to say these words to a woman who wasn't his lover and who was practically a stranger to him. But when for my own sanity I didn't turn up, he didn't come after me either. Though he was a fundamentally wordless man, the fragments of the few words ever spoken by him had grazed my flesh like shards of glass from a broken bottle. I was so afraid of the deadly power of words, I always, always preferred to joke.

8

As soon as I got back from overseas, I headed over to see my neighbor, Yoko, who had been picking up my mail for me. Yoko lived on what was practically a cliff; the steps up to the house from the road were dangerous and slippery, and I was always worried I'd fall. I hadn't been there for about six months, but still I was surprised to see that right on the top at the edge of the cliff there were two new houses under construction. The exterior walls were freshly painted and the sound of a drill or electric saw reverberated from the interior.

I pushed open her simple garden gate, which was no more than a couple of planks of wood nailed crosswise over a wooden frame. Yoko was in the corner of the garden, crouched over some small potted plants. She stood up and turned towards me, and I was momentarily stunned. Her face was that of an old woman.

A variety of large and small plant pots were scattered randomly around the tiny space that could barely be called a garden. Each one looked as if it had some kind of weed growing in it. I guessed they were some kind of rare wild grasses gathered from the neighboring mountains, or the side of the road somewhere.

"Are you on your own?" I asked.

"Tokiko was here but she just left," Yoko replied.

"Ah, too bad. I've got a souvenir for her too," I said, but Yoko didn't respond. She quickly rinsed off her hands under the outdoor faucet.

"Tokiko's boyfriend was over and they were upstairs listening to records, but then they went out driving somewhere," she said.

Yoko's daughter Tokiko was twenty and a senior at a two-year junior college, so of course she had a boyfriend with a car. I could easily imagine them listening to records upstairs, or for that matter, pretending to listen to records while they got up to something, and then probably going off in his car to his place and having sex there.

"She's a popular girl, your Tokiko. She always seems to have a boyfriend. Ever since she started high school you've been telling me about her and her boyfriends," I smiled, producing the red, brand-name wallet I'd bought for her at the duty-free.

"She's so good to these boys. She does everything for them. This one lives by himself, so I'm sure she's gone to cook dinner for him," said Yoko.

"I'm sorry all my gifts are from the duty-free," I said, handing Yoko a bottle of perfume. To tell the truth, perfume wasn't really something that I'd associate with Yoko.

Yoko stood there looking like an old woman. Yoko was still only forty years old.

Her long, black hair had lost its sheen and was liberally sprinkled with gray. She wore it tied back in a simple ponytail. Her face was covered in little grayish blotches and looked completely parched and weather-beaten—a scene of total devastation, unmitigated by any kind of protective cream or makeup.

"Is Hibiya-san out too?" I asked.

"My husband? Oh, he'll be back soon."

I'd brought a bottle of duty-free whiskey for her husband, Takuo Hibiya.

"You really shouldn't have. If Hibiya sets eyes on a bottle of whiskey he'll finish it off in one go," said Yoko, tucking the bottle behind the sofa.

Usually, she felt comfortable enough around me to call her husband "Takuo" or "Tak" but sometimes she referred to him by the more formal "Hibiya" or "my husband." But every time I heard the phrase *my husband* from her lips it made me recall the time twenty years ago when the twenty-year-old Yoko was about to become a young mother, and it sounded strange somehow.

Yoko's home was very small. The front door with its tiny entranceway opened directly into the living room and beyond that the kitchen. Off the kitchen was one more room, and that was it. The lone room on the second floor belonged to their daughter, Tokiko. The main space—the living room and kitchen—was cluttered but not dirty. There was a cheap-looking sofa and a low *kotatsu* table with an electric heater on the underside for keeping warm in the winter. I was sitting there now with my legs underneath.

"Hello there," Takuo called out as he came in.

I caught my breath. Takuo, too, was an old man. Elderly at forty. Had I really only been away for six months? I felt like Rip Van Winkle. I'd come to this house six months ago to ask Yoko to pick up my mail. At that time I'd thought that Yoko and Takuo had looked old, but only *looked*. Now they *were* old.

Takuo was wearing baggy black pants and a gray sweater, both of which were stained. His frizzy hair was down to the nape of his neck and graying, not evenly, but in patches. It made me think of dirty seaweed pulled from a winter sea.

"So how was it?" asked Takuo, drinking a glass of water in the kitchen.

"She brought us souvenirs," said his aged wife.

"Oh, thanks," said the aged husband, and with that, let himself out the tiny back door from the kitchen into the backyard. A few minutes passed but he didn't come back.

"Has Takuo gone out again?" I asked the elderly Yoko.

"No, he's just out in the back."

"The back?"

"You know that little prefab hut that parents set up for their kids to have a quiet place to study? Well he set one up for himself. Now, except for mealtimes, he's always in there," she explained.

"Is it big?"

"No, just one tiny room. Barely enough space to swing a cat," she answered, offering me a plate of cookies and rice crackers. "He doesn't ever clean up, and he's forbidden me to touch anything, so it just looks like a big trash can in there. You open the door and this terrible smell hits you, but he says he's fine with it. Tokiko won't go near the place. He wasn't here when Tokiko brought her boyfriend over today, which was fine. But if he's ever in the hut when her boyfriend comes over, he always seems to know. He comes in and complains to me later."

The old lady spoke slowly and calmly as if she were discussing a complete stranger. Her voice hadn't changed in twenty years. Back then, when I'd asked her how they were going to manage at their age with a baby to feed, she'd answered in that same slow, detached tone, "But there's nothing else for me to do in life but have babies."

"Do you have shopping to do? If you're on your way out, we can go together," I said, getting to my feet.

"The supermarket's closed today. That's why I'm at home," said Yoko, smiling.

Yoko had a part-time job at the local R—— mart.

Three years ago when Yoko told me they'd built and moved into this new house on top of a cliff, I'd been amazed. Of course, it wasn't surprising in itself that the couple who, twenty years ago, had been just twenty years old, had now made a family and built a house. It was that both husband and wife barely worked, but somehow they'd brought up a child, and now they had even managed to buy themselves a house.

As I was leaving, I wondered out loud what Takuo's secret hideout was like, and peeked out of the back door. It was a simple hut that looked like some sort of worker's bunkhouse, built almost right up against the house. Not a sound could be heard from it.

It was a beautiful day so I decided to visit H—— Archaeological Park instead of heading straight home. The main feature of the park was its reconstructions of Jomon-period dwellings. They were set on the sunny side of a hill; the view was fantastic and it was a pleasant, relaxing spot.

Besides the reconstructed homes, there were several archaeological remains of actual Jomon-period dwellings, each consisting of a ring of stones. Standing there, you could look out and see the gentle hills rolling away into the distance. After gradually hollowing out into a valley, the land rose gently up again to form another hill. On that next hill stood the H—— apartment complex. Then, on the one beyond that, was another similar structure that must have been the K—— apartment complex. A few degrees away from these, the land rose again in gradual waves up to a mound that resembled an ancient tumulus. At the base of that mound, the ground had been cut away to build two tennis courts.

H—— Archaeological Park was at an altitude of about 330 feet. Here and there in the narrow, elongated hills around it many different sites of Jomon-era remains had been unearthed. In the park stood a wooden notice board with information about all the sites that had been found. The ground beneath the K—— apartment complex had produced a multitude of earthenware and stone tools and other artifacts. I'd heard that there'd been similar sites under the H—— apartment complex. Both of the hills on which these complexes had been built sloped gently upwards and overlooked shallow valleys. There had been many such ancient settlements discovered in these hills but most had also vanished under housing developments.

I imagined long, long ago, these hills were covered in thick forest, and there would probably have been natural springs, rivers, or even small lakes in the valleys. All kinds of birds and other beasts would have converged here in search of water. The early humans who settled here would have found it ideal for catching fish and other animals for food, or for gathering nuts and berries. The remains of human dwellings, stone artifacts and pottery found here were all from the Jomon period or earlier. There was very little from the later, agricultural Yayoi period, probably because there was too little level ground in these hills and valleys suitable for the cultivation of rice. I couldn't quite get my head around the concept of *ten thousand years ago* or *seven thousand years ago* but what I did understand, I thought as I stood there looking out over the rolling hills and valleys bathed in soft, gentle sunlight, was why humans wanted to come and live in such a pleasant place.

Perhaps it was the sea that had come pouring over this land, creating its waves, or maybe the land itself had come pouring out from deep in the earth's core, but in much more recent years, this land of hills and valleys had supported another great influx, a surge of human beings from the big cities. These days, its waves were heaving with this new deluge of humanity.

I myself had moved to this land five years ago. Two years later, Yoko's family had followed the same route. The K—— apartment complex's residents had poured in fifteen or twenty years earlier, and those in the H—— and M—— apartment complexes too. Since then, many more people had whittled away at the hills and valleys to build their own homes. It wasn't because the location was ideal for hunting and gathering; it was that the land was still cheap.

The pot that Yoko had given me containing one of her unusual wild flowers hung at my side. I wasn't sure when it was that Yoko had become so enamored with plants. I had no idea whether she'd liked them as a child, but I knew that two decades ago the twenty-year-old, newly sexually active Yoko had eyes for nothing but her Takuo. The two had spent all their time entwined in each other, both physically and emotionally. The twenty-year-old father and mother got married because they'd made a child together. They had taken the money they got from the parents of the father and the parents of the mother, and cradled their downy-soft offspring like a baby doll, blissfully unconcerned with what tomorrow might bring.

9

Kumiko came over. I gave her a bottle of duty-free perfume too.

"Perfumes are only for admiring," she laughed, balancing the tiny bottle in the palm of her hand.

"Don't be so ungracious," I retorted. "Buying souvenirs for everyone was a tough job, so I decided to get everything all at once at the duty-free."

"When am I ever going to wear perfume?" asked Kumiko, a little sulkily.

"Anytime you feel like it! When you've got a hot date or something."

"What if the guy can't stand the smell of perfume?"

"Well if I were you, I'd do whatever you want," I said with a grin. "But then again I have to admit Japanese people don't have a strong smell so I suppose scent is hardly a necessity."

"Kyoko . . ." Kumiko began, but then suddenly stopped. I caught the expression on her face. "I'm having a baby."

"I see."

"Well, aren't you surprised?"

"Well, you did write in your letter that you wanted to have a child."

"But I'm not married."

"You can still have a baby if you're not married, you know."

"You know, that's what I hate about you, Kyoko. You're totally unshockable!" she said with a grin.

"*Whoa! I'm so shocked. Who's the father? When are you due?* Are those the kinds of thing I'm supposed to say? Don't tell me it's that big dumb guy's kid," I teased her back.

"Ah, big, dumb guy is so right. He really is dumb, that man. I've recently worked out that the stupidest people are the ones who have no idea of their own stupidity," said Kumiko with a laugh. "I've also realized that having that idiot's baby makes me an idiot too. Still, it follows that the fact I've realized I'm an idiot makes me less of an idiot than he is. But that big guy truly is a first-class idiot."

"You know, I really don't know. I'm not sure whether the big guy is a true idiot or not. He looks dumb but I believe he might actually have some thoughts in his head," I laughed.

"Yes, I think he has some," Kumiko agreed.

"That's right. We mustn't be misled that he's dumb just because of his size. It's not like he's some Neanderthal knuckle-dragger," I pointed out.

"Yeah, we wouldn't want to discriminate against Neanderthals," added Kumiko, playing the straight guy in our *manzai*-style comedy routine.

"Still, I bet he was exposed in all his idiotic glory when you told him you were pregnant."

"Yes, his idiocy was indeed fully exposed when it came to that topic," laughed Kumiko.

"In what way?"

"Of course he got all worked up. Said how he'd marry me. How he was going to divorce Ayako and stuff like that."

"But of course you told him that you had no intention of getting married."

"Yes, I even told him I didn't need him to acknowledge paternity."

"Of course, the big guy had no idea that you might get pregnant."

"Yes, well, I told him that I was on the pill, and he believed me."

"He must have been in total shock."

"He was surprised all right, but as always he expressed himself with that usual feigned politeness. It was quite funny."

According to Kumiko, Ayako was completely oblivious to all this. Kumiko was still helping Ayako and her friends with the Veggie Club. In fact, these days, she had become a key member of the club. Being a pharmacist, she had knowledge that was a huge help to them.

"I can see the big guy being shocked and totally freaking out, but what I can't understand is why you want to have his baby," I asked her.

"It's very simple. I just wanted to have a family."

"A family?"

"One person doesn't make a family. When my parents die I'll be all alone."

"So why not get married?"

"I don't think of that as a real family—like you, being married, but not having children. It's children that make a family."

"Then why don't you get married and have children?"

"I just don't like the institution of marriage. I've told you that enough times!" But this time, she didn't trot out all her old arguments.

I decided not to press further at that point, but still I couldn't understand why Kumiko was really going to have the baby of the man we called the big guy. The child's father was a big dumb guy. Even if she cut all ties with him by the time she had the child, even though the child would be a completely unique person, biologically speaking, he or she would still inherit something from the father. How would the whole paternity issue be handled? Would Kumiko convince herself that the child was the product of some kind of asexual, monogenetic reproduction? What if the child ended up resembling its father physically? If indeed she had consciously chosen the father of her child, it'd be more typical of Kumiko to choose an excellent specimen of masculinity to be the father, an alpha male, if you will. Could this man really be her alpha male?

"So does Ayako really look that much like you?" I asked, wanting to change the subject.

"Well we do look a bit alike on the outside, but of course our personalities are completely different," Kumiko replied.

"But you wrote that you were almost identical."

"I thought that you'd find that amusing to read way over there in your foreign country."

"What? You made it all up? Don't tell me the jogging bit was a lie too!"

"But you loved it, didn't you? Ayako is the kind of person who believes it's safer to stick to the stereotypical role laid out for married women. And both husband and wife are all about playing it safe, right? So when the two are alone together they don't have anything to talk about. Whenever I was there, it seemed like Ayako was relieved to have a diversion. I don't get their relationship at all. They're completely bored, but for the sake of peace and security, they don't give a hint of it. Or maybe in fact Ayako isn't bored at all . . ." Kumiko's expression was serious.

"What would Ayako do if she knew you were having a baby?"

"I told her from the time we first met that I had a boyfriend. Sometimes I even make up stories about him. I know how to play it safe too, you know! Once I've had the baby I'm going to have nothing more to do with that couple. I'm going to move somewhere far away."

"Kumiko, you are a piece of work! So what's this so-called boyfriend like?"

"A year older than me, we met at university, he's handsome, works in a hospital," said Kumiko, grinning mischievously.

In contrast, I was inwardly grimacing. I really thought she had gone too far. It was true that when I first met Kumiko three years earlier, she was already talking of becoming a single mother. But now it looked as though her dreams were about to become reality.

I had long since lost all interest in the man, but the mixture of Kumiko's fictitious stories and now her supposed "true story" had piqued my curiosity about Ayako, the woman who was his wife. I was interested in the security of this woman called Ayako. No, rather, I was interested in breaching this security.

"Did you really visit Ayako's house like you wrote in your letters? Do you still go there now?" I asked.

"I went there two or three times, I guess. I still go by every so often to pick up vegetables. It'd be suspicious to suddenly stop going altogether."

"Does Ayako ever come by your place?"

"For Veggie Club."

"Would you mind if I was there one time? When Ayako drops by?"

"No way. I know you. You're planning to give the game away."

"Boy, you're quick. You're smarter than you look," I laughed.

"You know, I wouldn't mind if it was you who ratted me out. The only person besides me who could possibly rat us out to Ayako is the big guy. And clearly neither of us is going to tell. Still, somebody has to do it, and there's no better person for the job than you, Kyoko," Kumiko joked.

"You and I, we really don't like things to be too peaceful, do we?" I laughed.

"Isn't it ironic that these pacifists have to fight for their peace?" said Kumiko, with amusement.

I didn't mention Kumiko's obvious anxiety. Kumiko in turn didn't mention my headaches. I already felt the iron band around my head beginning to loosen.

10

Yoko's husband, Takuo, had a temporary job shifting earth at a dig site in the small town of Z—— chō, on the far north side of the K—— apartment complex. His job was to remove earth from the sites of excavations that were being done there. Apparently, there had long been plans to build a huge housing complex in the hills of Z——. Fifteen years previously, there had been an investigation underway by the Archaeology department of some local university, checking out the land for ancient remains. But it had been put on hiatus five years in, and then restarted seven years ago. So, Takuo had explained to Yoko, they were now in phase two of the research project, and it was almost complete. This meant we'd have to go now if we wanted to visit the site before bulldozers moved in to level the ground in preparation for construction. But neither Yoko nor Tokiko had any interest in going all the way out to Z—— to see the excavation.

"The pay's lousy, but at least he's working," said Yoko, whose sole concern was that her husband had a job.

Tokiko just stood by her mother and smiled.

"So where is this junior college you go to, Tokiko?" I asked. The address was some town I'd never heard of.

For no apparent reason this caused Yoko to chuckle to herself before telling me the address again. The name of the town sounded vaguely like a Western person's name and yet at the same time also had an ancient Japanese feel to it. It was completely mysterious to me. She explained that this was a very recently built college, up in the mountains on the border with the next prefecture, and difficult to get to. Of course, Tokiko had ended up at this obscure, inconveniently located school because she hated studying and her high school grades had been so poor.

Tokiko didn't speak at all except to respond to a direct question. She just stood there smiling. She had an endearing face, and an overall gentle demeanor. She was of average height and build—a universally likeable type of girl.

"Tokiko, you must be extremely popular," I commented.

"No, not really," she replied, beaming.

Her way of speaking and her gestures were those of a typical junior college student, yet somehow there was an undertone of something indecent. Unwittingly, this twenty-year-old young woman gave off a kind of vaporous aura of sexuality—it enveloped her whole body like a sort of filmy membrane. Maybe it was because she was standing right by her mother, but the aura seemed to engulf Yoko too, and her tired expression seemed far more animated than usual.

"Is your husband at the construction site every day?"

"No, not every day. Not when it's raining. He just used to go when he got a call from the university professor or the administrator. But he's finished now."

What on earth could Takuo Hibiya find to do out in that hut all day long?

"I brought you one of the daikon radishes that came today from the Veggie Club," said Yoko, producing a mud-encrusted object from a bag and placing it by my back door.

"Oh, so you're a member of the Veggie Club too?"

"Yes, a neighbor from one of the houses down the hill recommended it. She's the neighborhood rep for the club. It turns out it's all pretty good—the leafy greens, the root vegetables—all of it. And it's good for your health. My neighbor says that since she started eating Veggie Club produce she hasn't caught so much as a cold, and her digestion is working much better than before. And because they deliver so much, you end up eating lots of healthy vegetables," Yoko explained to me earnestly. She displayed a kind of passion that I had never seen from her.

Throughout this explanation, Tokiko stood arm in arm with her mother, her body turned slightly towards hers. Her faintly pink, glowing complexion was enveloped by the thin, vaporous film, and she looked to me like a young girl standing on the bank of a lake, obscured by mist. The whole time I was talking to Yoko, Tokiko stood in the mist, faintly smiling. The twenty-year-old resembled neither her father nor her mother. She was like an anonymous presence standing quietly by. Yet this presence managed to capture my attention more than her mother did. Perhaps this was because the aura made her skin seem to shimmer.

"Where are you off to?" I asked.

"Tokiko was going clothes shopping and she asked me to keep her company," answered Yoko, again giving a strange little laugh in the back of her throat. Her muffled voice resonated with happiness. Or perhaps it was more like the sound of a delighted animal.

I wondered whether, twenty years from now, Tokiko would become Yoko. If the daughter would become the mother and the mother would disappear entirely. No, I thought, this mother would stand beside her daughter, now a mother herself, and would chuckle deep in the back of her throat. And then would the daughter of her daughter also stand there smiling, her body leaning in towards her mother's? All three women would line up, shoulder to shoulder to shoulder . . .

Although not visible, perhaps Yoko's own mother was also standing there with them.

"Tokiko's quite rich, you know. She has a part-time job, and her grandmother sends her an allowance." Yoko chuckled yet again, and looked at Tokiko tenderly as if to feed her happiness.

"In our house, she's the only one with any cash. Her grandmother pays her college tuition too. She sends Takuo and me food and clothes from time to time, but recently she's stopped sending us any living expenses. So we have the things we need, but no spare cash. Tokiko's the only rich one."

By the cheerful way she reported all this, Yoko appeared perfectly content with the situation.

"Is your husband home today?" I asked.

"Hmm, I guess he's probably around somewhere. Did you see him?" she asked, turning to look at Tokiko, but the girl's expression didn't change.

I assumed Takuo Hibiya could only have been paid an hourly wage for the temporary excavation work—just a little spare cash.

He'd picked up different kinds of day labor over the years, and would probably do so again in the future. Yoko was only making pocket money at her part-time job at the supermarket. And yet they had built a house and their daughter was doing well for herself at a private junior college.

"We've got cats now. Would you like to come over and see them?" asked Tokiko with her perpetual beam.

"Someone abandoned one right in front of the house so I brought it in, and Tokiko bought the other one," explained the euphoric mother.

"So you've got two to look after."

"But they're both so cute, aren't they?" Yoko looked at her daughter, who nodded in agreement.

"I'd love to see them."

So, in addition to the family of three, the house on the cliff had acquired two more residents.

After my visitors left, I took a walk to the big bookstore by the T——train station. As I entered, I spotted Takuo over in the travel section, his nose in a book. I walked right by him but he was so engrossed in his book that he didn't notice me, and I decided not to speak to him. As I passed, I saw that he was holding a large color-illustrated guide book to Paris with a glossy photo of the Eiffel Tower on the cover. His brow was furrowed, and he was glaring so hard at a map of Paris that he could have been gazing upon the gates of hell.

After wandering around the store, asking after a couple of books and leafing through a few magazine articles, I eventually made it back to the door. Takuo was still staring at the map of Paris. He looked for all the world like a post-war homeless man squatting in the underground passages of Tokyo. His hair and beard were wild and unkempt, he looked as if he hadn't washed his face in days and he was still dressed in his stained sweater and dirty, threadbare pants. Slung over his shoulder was a kind of canvas sack, identical to the kind of oversized cloth bags used by the homeless to carry all their personal effects.

"Hibiya-san!" I called to him from a slight distance.

"Hi," he answered, blinking repeatedly as if trying to refocus.

"I just had a visit from your wife and daughter," I said.

"Really?" he answered, his mind clearly still occupied by the streets of Paris.

"Are the remains at Z—— still open to the public?" I asked.

"Actually we finished up there two months ago."

"So they're off-limits now?"

"No, I think it's still okay to visit."

"What are you doing for work these days?"

"Nothing."

"Are you off to Paris?"

"Yes. Well, I'd sure like to go."

When I looked into Takuo's eyes, it was a map of Parisian streets that I saw reflected there. His wife and daughter were nowhere to be seen. The forty-year-old husband and father with a body hunched over like an old man and a sallow, grimy complexion was dreaming only of the streets of a faraway country.

"They say that the Z—— remains are amazing. What do you think?"

"They're big. We pretty much dug up the whole hill."

"Was it fascinating?"

"I was just moving the earth."

"Right. Anyway, I think I'll go and take a look soon. Well, see you."

I set off home, leaving Takuo to his guide book.

I really didn't know anything about Takuo. Even twenty years ago, he was a mystery to me. He hadn't seemed particularly eccentric. He had a wife and a child. Whenever he had a job, he would work. Sometimes he would quit that job, but he would always find himself a new one. Takuo certainly wasn't lazy. He simply had never become a regular salaryman.

After leaving Takuo in the bookstore, it suddenly struck me as strange that this man was father to Tokiko. Takuo was practically the same age as me, yet he didn't seem like a man, or a father. As I thought back on Tokiko and her cheerful face, it seemed more and more as though Takuo were vanished or dead. A parent who had raised a child, and then died. It was as if he inhabited the afterworld.

11

Kumiko called and asked me to come over. It was the first time I'd been to her new place. It turned out to be in an upscale, three-story red brick apartment building. Her apartment was on the first floor and included a small grass lawn in the backyard.

"Ayako's coming over with some vegetables," Kumiko explained when I arrived.

So Kumiko had specifically asked me over to meet Ayako.

Kumiko went outside and stood barefoot on the grass. There was a chain-link fence dividing the yard from the street, a trailing rose entwined in its mesh.

"Kyoko!" she called back to me, "Look, mole holes!"

Also barefoot, I followed her out onto the lawn. She was pointing to an area covered in holes, but whether they were made by a mole or not, I had no idea. For some reason Kumiko was in high spirits today. She called out "Ayako!" and waved, putting one foot up on the fence as if about to climb it.

"Ayako's here," she said, and crossed by me to meet her at the front. Kumiko was wearing wide-leg culottes and as she passed by I could feel the breeze she stirred up.

I heard Kumiko, and what must have been Ayako's voice, at the front door. Ayako had noticed that Kumiko had a guest, and was apologizing repeatedly for her intrusion. Meanwhile, Kumiko was repeatedly urging her to come inside. After a while, they both came out into the yard. Ayako looked nothing like Kumiko—not even a little bit. Admittedly, they both had short, straight haircuts, but Ayako's style was very simple, like that of an elementary-school girl, while Kumiko's was very fashionably cut. Their faces weren't similar either. Even their builds were completely different. Ayako was much shorter than Kumiko. So this was the big guy's financial controller, the woman who responded to everything with "Sounds great!" The frigid one.

Kumiko introduced me. Ayako offered me the appropriate greeting. I responded in kind.

"How's Katsumi?" Kumiko inquired.

"He's at home," Ayako replied, and her tone was exactly the one that her husband had used for reporting to me what his wife had said.

"On such a beautiful day?" asked Kumiko.

"He's watching TV," said Ayako. With Kumiko, she spoke like a close friend. Her tone changed when she addressed me. It was the first time we'd met, so she was very polite, and I was the same. However, it was extremely difficult for me to make small talk with this woman.

"Do you really deliver all this heavy stuff by yourself?" I asked her, glancing at the cardboard box of vegetables by the front door.

"There's not usually so much. Kumiko didn't come by to pick up her veggies last time, so this is two weeks' worth. She usually comes to my apartment to get them. I have a small family too, so we normally get one delivery and split it, but Kumiko says even that's too much for her . . ."

There was absolutely no other topic for me to broach with Ayako, nor did she attempt to start any conversation with me. It would be fair to say that she was exactly like her husband in this respect. She said nothing that wasn't necessary. It was hard for me to believe that Kumiko could be so close with this woman, even so far as to share a Veggie Club portion.

"Well, Kumiko really isn't supposed to carry heavy things right now," I said, deliberately concealing my glee under a serious expression.

"Is she sick?" Ayako asked me.

"Apparently she's pregnant."

"Oh, so that's it," said Ayako, looking at the floor. Then suddenly she asked Kumiko, "Does my husband know?"

"Why? It's nothing to do with Katsumi. How could he know?" she answered.

"Right, of course," mumbled Ayako.

"So your children must be in middle or high school?" I asked. Kumiko shot me a look.

"Kumiko, I'm expecting someone from the Veggie Club to come by, so I really can't stay," said Ayako hurriedly. She left without touching the fruit and yogurt plate that Kumiko had put out for us all.

"You went too far, Kyoko," said Kumiko angrily, the minute she was gone.

"Well, obviously your advance publicity regarding your so-called boyfriend didn't have any effect. Ayako clearly knows you're going to have her husband's baby," I retorted. I was just as angry as Kumiko was.

"But asking her if her kids are in middle or high school. That's just mean."

"But I'm not supposed to know whether or not she's got kids."

"You're horrible."

"Why?"

"You know why."

"Tell me why."

"Look, they're married. She must have wanted kids. Not everyone's like you. You're the one who's a freak, so don't go around judging every other woman by your own standards. It's abnormal not to have children. As for Ayako . . ."

Kumiko was unable to say another word; she was so filled with fury at me.

"It's great that everyone has their own hopes and dreams. I guess for someone like Ayako she really needed to have children to fulfill hers," I shrugged, going back out onto the lawn. I crouched down to examine the holes that might or might not have been mole holes.

"Kyoko!" Kumiko's voice above my head felt powerful enough to crush me into the earth. "Even you weren't always so sure what you wanted."

I didn't say anything.

"Go on, tell me why. What's the reason you're so alone?" she continued.

"I'm not alone. I'm married, aren't I?" I directed my answer to the holes in the lawn.

"You're not being honest, Kyoko."

On the other side of the street, I could see a large cherry tree. The blossom buds were still tightly closed, but even from a distance I could see that the tips had turned from a reddish brown to a pinkish color. One of the thickest branches hung low, almost parallel to the ground. Three little girls, around six or seven in age, were playing a game to see who could fly the farthest. They stepped up using a concrete block, jumped to grasp hold of the branch, then swung like gymnasts on a horizontal bar before launching themselves into the air, their skirts flying.

"That's dangerous," said Kumiko, approaching the fence. "That branch is really starting to bend. If they swing like that, it's going to break. It's really . . . Hey, that's dangerous!" she yelled across to the girls.

The three girls glanced over, but completely ignored Kumiko's warning. They hung on the branch and continued to swing back and forth.

"That's dangerous!" called Kumiko one more time.

I also thought the girls' game was dangerous. I had been on the point of getting to my feet and shouting at them too, but I stayed crouched down. From a crouching position, you couldn't hear the girls' voices. From the level of the holes in the lawn, you couldn't hear a thing.

I too could have died before the age of six or seven. There was a long scar at the top of one of my thighs. It was from an incision made to remove an infection I'd gotten following a vaccination. I'd also had my tonsils removed at the age of six or seven. During that operation, there had been some kind of slip-up, and I almost hadn't made it. So I could easily have died back then. And I had, in fact, fallen on my head once after a tree branch broke while I was playing with friends, trying to see who could jump the farthest.

I was trying to die along with the little girls. I'd have to swing my body as hard as I could, way up into the sky. If I only swung a little, the fall wouldn't kill me. *Swing harder! Let's swing higher . . . Higher! Higher! Let's disappear into the sky, far, far away from the Earth. Higher! Higher!* I stared deep into the holes in the ground as I worked my incantation. If those little girls didn't fall to their death, then my childhood self wouldn't be able to die either. The cherry tree branch had to snap.

Kumiko was talking to me.

"You really do despise Katsumi, don't you? I could tell from your attitude to Ayako. You could only have been that awful to her if you had no respect for her husband either. Why do you hate him so much? I don't see anything about him that deserves that much scorn. I don't understand what's not to like about him. He's just a regular guy. There are literally millions of regular guys like him in the world. Big, healthy, entirely without cynicism—a straightforward, decent person. I know this sounds like I'm talking about an animal or a vegetable, but genetically there's nothing wrong with him. I just don't see what you find so objectionable."

"It looks like it's going to be a very bleak Sunday at Ayako's place. How is she going to bring up such an unpleasant topic? How's the big guy going to handle it? The very thing they've been avoiding ever since they got married is now finally unavoidable. Ayako will no longer be able to say 'Sounds great! See you later, then!' And the big guy won't be able to smile politely and feel utterly secure. I'd love to see it."

"I get it. You can't stand peace and security. You only derive pleasure from war and destruction," said Kumiko, who couldn't help smiling.

"War is harsh, but total peace can be just as harsh. Those two and their naïve wanting to get all worked up over beautiful things are the same. They're more into that than the important stuff—like being concerned about this child."

I was thinking of the forty-two-year-old man who stood on the beach staring at the starry sky and fantasizing about his lover.

The little girls had given up cheating death on the branch of a cherry tree, and had started a game of Chinese jump rope. The two holding the elastic around their legs moved it higher and higher. The girl in the middle jumped and tried to land on the elastic. Then they gradually lowered it again. Next, they all began a counting chant with the elastic at knee height and the girl in the middle jumped over each side in turn. Somehow, the whole maneuver had the air of something more complex than a little kid's game.

"There's going to be bloodshed at Ayako's place," said Kumiko looking into the distance.

"No, there's going to be nothing of the sort. Those two don't even possess the ability to have a good argument."

"Kyoko, why do you look down on those two? You shouldn't underestimate them. They're much stronger than you are."

"Well, that's obvious. And that's why you've decided to get me to be your accomplice in all this. I know perfectly well that the big guy isn't the father of your baby. You know what—you're masterminding this whole thing!" I said, grinning.

I didn't really know whether Kumiko's baby was the big guy's or even the supposedly fictional boyfriend's. I had no way of checking whether the fictional boyfriend actually existed, and I had no intention of poking my nose in that far. Even if the baby turned out to be the big guy's, he was no longer involved at all.

"The big guy is just a regular guy. I know he doesn't have a bad bone in his body. I don't know why it is, but the more time anyone spends with him, the more unpleasant it makes them," said Kumiko, her expression somber. Then she realized how serious she was being and began to laugh.

Realizing that Kumiko and I felt the same way, I burst out laughing too.

Anybody living their ordinary everyday life likes to escape into the extraordinary from time to time. Going on a trip is one example. Because you know that you'll be coming back, you can feel safe embarking on the journey. But a journey without a return portion is a journey that turns into your everyday life. It becomes the new "ordinary" rather than an escape into the "extraordinary." It's the same with a festival or a party. If every day were a party, then it wouldn't be a party anymore. For that big guy, every day was ordinary. The expression of a person's sexuality should be like a journey or a party. It's the extraordinary in the midst of all the ordinary. But as if sex were some kind of close encounter with death, the man had tried to wrap the extraordinariness of sex inside a protective coating of ordinariness. All of that "cute face" "you feel just right," and "you're just the right height" nonsense were his standards of normalcy. By measuring extraordinary or special things by these yardsticks, he was dulling their sheen with the drab paint of ordinariness and routine. He never took that blind, yet exhilarating, leap into the extraordinary and the unknown. Even with sex, he would never take any risks. He was a man who did everything he could to avoid the pain of everyday living, but because he was so successful at avoiding it, he never felt any need for the escape of something extraordinary or amazing.

Yet, that big guy had once stood on a beach under a starry sky and dreamed up a lover. He had stood at the foot of the bridge to old age and forced himself to dream.

Kumiko, at least, didn't have to come face to face with old age yet.

"Hey, you know that steep slope on the way back to your house? That beautiful part with oaks and beeches? That's the way I always used to go to see you. Did you know they've built some houses there? They've cut down all the trees and replaced them with single-family homes. I think there are eight of them in all," Kumiko told me.

"Yes, I've seen them. They were selling for fifty million yen each. There was a signboard up with the layout and price of each."

"Well, one of my old friends from university is living in one of them. She asked me to drop by today for her housewarming. She's got two kids. Actually, she claims the house is a bit small for a family of four."

"Yes, they all look very nice from the outside, but I thought they didn't look very big. Pretty expensive for what you get."

"Still, all eight were sold."

"So your friend has two children. I wonder why these days stopping at two children suddenly seems to be all the rage?" I asked, playfully, as if posing a riddle.

"Homes are small? School fees are high?" offered Kumiko.

"I'm sure that's part of it, but don't you think it's so the whole family can fit comfortably into one car?" I suggested with a smile.

"But you can get three people in the back."

"Yes, but the compact models only seat four."

"I see. If you have five children, you have to buy two cars. Yes, you may be right. It's all about seating capacity," giggled Kumiko.

"Everything's about cars these days. Cars and dining tables—they all seat four. Five has become an odd number. All my neighbors have two kids. Or just one."

"Now that you mention it, all of my married college friends have two children. Usually one boy and one girl."

Kumiko and I walked up to the hill that used to be woodlands and now was the site of eight brand-new houses. I used to stand in those woods and watch the sun go down behind the houses on the next hill. There'd been not only the familiar magpies, bulbuls, doves, and sparrows but other species living there too, whose names I didn't know.

The white walls of the new houses reflected the evening sun and it looked as if the whole area had been tinted reddish-gold. The house belonging to Kumiko's friend was the last one, right at the top of the steep slope. All the homes faced the street and had tiny gardens in front. The trees planted in these gardens were still ridiculously, almost apologetically tiny little saplings. What appeared to be the living rooms could be entered by sliding glass doors. White lace curtains hung at each pane. A car was squeezed into the tiny space in front of each house. In some of the houses, the lights were on and you could see people moving around beyond the lace curtains.

I wondered if there were ancient human dwellings deep in the ground of this hill too.

"These are lovely houses. It must be nice to live in a brand-new home," I remarked.

"But my friend told me it's tough. Everyone had to take out a huge loan to buy their house. Even with the loan, my friend and her husband couldn't really afford a place like this as they're still only in their thirties. It sounds like his parents are rich or something, but even so, she tells me, they can only really save money each month by cutting down on their food expenses. From the outside they may look rich, but it's a different story inside," explained Kumiko, stopping and looking across at the next hill.

I stood next to her, watching the sun's afterglow as it slipped behind the crest of the hill.

"I'll bet the view was fantastic back in the Jomon period and that the land was expensive then too. Look at this place! There's a river right over there, a valley nearby—it's a great location. There must have been plenty of wild boars to eat. I'll bet the Jomon real estate agents drew their clients' attention to all of that," I joked.

The houses had been built on both sides of the newly created road—four on each side. On one side, there was still some trace of the woods that used to be there. I was sure there were two parents and two children inside each house. On weekends, did they all jump into the car squeezed into the narrow space by the front door and go wild boar-hunting? Or fishing? Or nut and berry-gathering? Or fetching water from the river? No, the men of the family probably did all their hunting on weekdays.

"Amiko!" called Kumiko to the woman who stepped out to greet us.

"I wondered where you were," said the woman called Amiko.

There were white walls, white curtains, and a white-painted wooden picket fence. Even the car was off-white. Brushing aside my attempts to make my apologies and leave, Kumiko and Amiko took me by the arm and led me inside. I saw a girl of about five or six and a boy of three or four, but they both quickly fled from the room. There was also a man in his mid-thirties, wearing a light cardigan, apparently Amiko's husband.

"I thought I'd find out what you wanted before getting you a housewarming present," said Kumiko. Amiko's husband expertly removed the cork from a bottle of wine.

"Cheers," he said, and we drank a toast.

"We don't know anyone in the neighborhood so I'm really glad you came too," said Amiko, refilling my glass.

The children reappeared.

"Eri-chan!" said her father, going over to his daughter. He put his arm around her shoulder affectionately and whispered something in her ear. The girl had an angelic expression on her face, but it was clear that the expression was specially put on for the occasion. Then, she whispered something in her father's ear, took hold of her little brother's hand, and led him away. Perhaps it was a strategy of the father's to make sure the kids stayed out of the way until the guests were gone. It was through the pink hue of my glass of rosé that I watched the little girl whose name was Eri take her little brother's hand and disappear. As Eri was leaving, the father winked at the children's mother. The mother shrugged her shoulders and chuckled in amusement. I envied little Eri, but I can't say I envied her parents.

12

Yoko had been trying zealously to recruit me into the Veggie Club. Her recruitment methods reminded me of the way religious cults try to induct new members. I suppose it was because Yoko truly believed in the Veggie Club produce. Organic Produce was her idol, her object of devotion.

She started by telling me that her "idol" was the most delicious. But as taste is not only an abstract concept, but in the end totally subjective, there was no use in this approach. Naturally, she preached next how the produce was without chemical contamination. As this was only secondhand information that she had learned somewhere, she wasn't very persuasive. I wasn't all that well-informed myself, but I was already aware that chemicals, and not only agricultural chemicals such as pesticides, could be harmful.

"Now that you mention it, I remember all the fuss over fish being contaminated with PCBs, but these days you don't hear anything about it any more," I said, but as vegetables were Yoko's object of worship, she had no interest in talking about fish.

"Doesn't it give you roundworms?" I asked, examining the leaves of the fresh vegetables she'd brought over.

"No, there's nothing like that in them!" she cheerfully assured me.

"Well, I don't suppose anyone's going to complain," I laughed.

"No, I've never heard anyone complain about that—roundworms," replied Yoko.

"When I was a kid I was always getting roundworms. One time I had about six of them in me." I had no desire to elaborate any further than that.

In fact, I had been made to drink a kind of deworming medicine. Then, the next day I had to lay several sheets of newspaper on the floor and defecate on them. The newspaper system was for ease of checking whether the worms had been evacuated or not. Toilets were not the flushing kind that we have nowadays, but a deep hole in the ground, so this was the only way to see.

My mother had told me that the worms were in my stomach, living on my blood.

They're taking away important nutrition from you. That's why you look so pale, why you have no energy, why you just want to sleep all the time. It's the worms in your stomach doing that.

As a child, I had visions of these worms in my stomach, their tight little mouths sucking on my red blood, stealing all of my food. Sometimes I felt stabbing pains, sometimes more of a griping or wrenching, and I was always convinced that this was the worms wriggling around inside my stomach. I became consumed with fear that they were happily drinking up all of my blood.

The only way to free myself of such terrors was to close my eyes and force down a bitter infusion made from a kind of seaweed, or to drink castor oil, a stinky concoction that made me want to throw up. In my child's mind, I believed that if I didn't drink these, the worms would succeed in draining me completely of blood and I would die. Still, it wasn't so much the abstract notion of death that frightened me, as the concrete vision of the worms wriggling around gape-mouthed inside my stomach that caused me mind-numbing terror.

In those days, there was always someone in my family who had worms. Our kitchen always seemed to be filled with the reek of steeping seaweed. Sometimes we were fed it mixed into sweet rice cakes in the hope of sugar-coating its foul taste. Other times we had to drink a medicine called *Makunin* made from the weed *makuri*. Grown-ups would tell us how lucky we were that we only had roundworms.

So-and-so next door has tapeworms, and those are really difficult to get rid of. Tapeworms are really long, so to get rid of them he has to get down on all fours so his parents can wind them around wooden chopsticks and pull them out.

I was told that tapeworms could actually be yards long. I couldn't bear to think what would happen if worms like that were slithering around inside me. Every household was struggling to make ends meet in those postwar days, and so they grew their own vegetables on whatever empty ground they could find. For fertilizer they used human waste, which was of course teeming with the eggs of these creatures.

"So what's Tokiko up to today?" I asked brightly, trying to banish the memory of the terrifying worms.

"Oh, she's gone to see a movie with her boyfriend," replied Yoko with her usual chuckle.

"Do you ever go out with Takuo?" I asked.

"With my husband? No, it's been five or six years since I went anywhere with him."

"Then you should find yourself a new boyfriend to go out with," I teased.

"Well, I . . . Oh, those days are long gone."

"What? You're still young!"

Yoko stared at me in bewilderment. I wondered if parents died the moment their child came of age.

"You know, that Katsumi-san is very dedicated to the Veggie Club," said Yoko.

"Katsumi?"

"He lives in the K—— apartment complex. He's recruited a lot of members."

"Surely you mean his wife?"

"Yes, that's it. Katsumi-san's wife."

"That man . . ."

"Do you know him?"

"Er, slightly."

"It seems there have been loads of new members from the K—— apartment complex recently. I heard it's all due to Katsumi-san's wife."

"Look, Yoko, you need to do like Tokiko and get yourself a boyfriend who'll take you to the movies," I said suddenly. Yoko just stared.

Even Yoko had to admit that "Katsumi's wife's" dedication to the Veggie Club and her enthusiastic recruitment of new members was rather like a church missionary's. Apparently, Ayako thought nothing of spending a whole Sunday saving hordes of souls by persuading them to eat those vegetables. Among the housewives per-suaded to join by Ayako's fervor were those who were also ready to take up the good fight and turn it into their new passion.

Once their children grow up, many Japanese homemakers take up some kind of hobby. They sign up for self-enrichment classes such as silk-rope braiding, artificial-silk or paper flower mak-ing, clay flower sculpting, wooden-doll making, or wickerwork. Usually they don't stick with it for long. However those who join "The Veggie Club" discover a whole new reason for living, and become devout followers like Ayako.

"Whatever you say, this does have an effect on your life," said Yoko.

The beauty of braided ropes, artificial flowers, and dolls won't improve your health, but vegetables have a real effect on your life. So you have a genuine reason to devote yourself to the cause. Was that really true?

"I quit smoking, too," Yoko announced.

"Well, I suppose if you inhale poison daily it doesn't make any difference whether your vegetables are poison-free or not," I said cheerfully. "And while they're at it, why don't they make a Rice Club, or a Fish Club, or a Meat Club? They really ought to buy a desert island and create a new, poison-free world on it," I added, causing Yoko to give her throaty chuckle.

In the end, despite Yoko's fervent pleas, I refused to join the Veggie Club. Missionaries like Ayako or Yoko were able to pour their heart and soul into it, and feel they were being useful to themselves, to their families, to others, and indeed to the whole of mankind. Because they were doing something of use, they were able to deliver to their members a purpose for living along with their box of veggies. It wasn't enough for them just to be alive. Personally, I believe in just living. If anything, I would like to pour my own heart and soul into achieving an even greater state of just living.

13

Kumiko and I made plans to go and visit the archaeological excavations in Z——. Actually, Kumiko was more interested in checking out the location of the massive housing complex that was going up there.

She turned up at my place in an off-white car. Her friend Amiko was driving but, at first glance, I mistook it for the big guy's car. The first time he had come to pick me up, he had made me this generous offer: *Anytime you need a ride somewhere don't waste your money on a taxi fare—just give me a call!*

"I ordered us a special taxi," said Kumiko, grinning.

"Bet you haven't seen many women cab drivers," said Amiko.

"Trouble is, this driver has no idea where she's going," said Kumiko.

"Not to worry—I know the way," I assured them. I was pretty sure I could remember the roads in the area from when I was driving around with the big guy. I recalled that sense of excitement I'd felt the first time I rode in the big guy's car, that I was embarking on some kind of forbidden journey. Already a year had passed since then.

"I've heard there are prehistoric dig sites all over this area," said Amiko.

The Amiko I'd visited at her home had seemed like the archetypal full-time mom, but today at the wheel of a car, dressed all in white and wearing trendy sunglasses, she looked chic and stylish. Kumiko had brought along a map and I spread it out on my lap and leaned forward from the backseat to give directions.

"I can't believe how hilly it is around here. We used to live in Hokkaido. Up there, you can travel as far as you like in a straight line and it'll always be completely flat. It was quite an adjustment for us to move somewhere like this," said Amiko.

"And you must have been really surprised when you bumped into your old college pal living close by," said Kumiko.

"Not to mention that after not seeing her for so long she also happens to be pregnant. I nearly fell over with shock," Amiko said.

"So it's true then?" I asked Kumiko.

"What? You didn't believe me?" she asked in mock indignation.

"I only half believed it. And you have to admit your stomach doesn't seem to have gotten any bigger," I pointed out.

"You see, that's the trouble with people who have never had children. They think the minute you get pregnant you blow up like a balloon," said Kumiko.

The car was passing by the K—— apartment complex. The road was unnecessarily wide right here.

"That big guy goes out for drives too, doesn't he?" I addressed my question to Kumiko but she didn't respond.

"I heard that before they built the K—— apartment complex they uncovered some ancient remains, and that it was the same case with all the housing complexes around here. The very first ones were found at the T——apartment complex," said Amiko.

"You're very well-informed," I commented.

"My husband was interested, so the other day he bought a pamphlet about it from the cultural center," she explained.

Kumiko was staring into space. Her face looked yellowish. For some reason I suddenly imagined we were riding in the big guy's car.

"You know, once a month at the cultural center they have lectures on the remains they've found. The talks on the history of the region are pretty interesting. They believe that Z——was the site of an ancient village. They found lots of Jomon-period relics there. They even think that Z——was an ancient clan name and that the village was named after the clan's headman," I told Amiko. This was the lecture I'd heard the day I met the big guy.

"I looked at the pictures of the excavation sites in the pamphlet my husband picked up. I couldn't believe some of the photos were supposed to be stone artifacts they dug up there. My husband laughed at me and told me I had no imagination, but when I saw the fragments of stone that they were supposed to have used to cut the flesh of animals or strip their pelts, I said they just looked like any old rocks you might see lying around."

"Amazing, huh?" I said laughing along with Amiko. Kumiko didn't join in.

"I guess you have to see the real thing, not just photos or diagrams," I went on. "I think I bought the same pamphlet. The lecturers explained it so that it made more sense. I used to think that Stone-Age dwellers used some random stone or piece of rock that they found lying around, but that's apparently not the case. They used to break up the rocks using other rocks, and then use the sharpest edge as a cutting tool. There were even tools that looked like spoons. It's really hard to believe, isn't it?"

"Right, let's decide not to believe until we see it for ourselves," laughed Amiko.

The light joking and laughter made for pleasant conversation. I recalled how this kind of pleasant conversation was exactly what I'd been hoping for at that first meal when I met the big guy, and continued to hope for every time after that when we went driving around.

"According to the map, we have to turn right here," I said, as we approached a side road.

We turned off the new road that had been built over the old Edo-period highway, and found ourselves driving through a convoluted maze of roads that sloped sharply up and down. I could hardly believe that people had built homes on this kind of mountainous terrain, but we passed through several residential neighborhoods before the road sloped sharply up to the ridge of the hill. From here on, the road was really just an access road for the large trucks that had begun construction work at the site. We parked the car and continued on foot.

We crossed the access road, pushed our way through an area of brush, and suddenly there below us was red earth stretching far into the distance.

"Incredible!" said Kumiko, sounding a little angry.

"It's far bigger than I imagined," I said, looking down on it in awe.

Already, nothing remained of the archaeological dig site that had been here. The new, red-colored earth that was shipped in had already been crushed and leveled by the bulldozers. The three of us stood side by side, shocked to witness the brutal, massive scale of "development" required in preparation for this grand construction project. Yet, more impressive was that, far and beyond the expanses of fresh, red earth and the denuded areas of black earth, hill upon hill rolled away into the distance as far as the eye could see, all as yet untouched by human hand.

"Look, over there, just below that wooded area. Can you see that big pond?" asked Amiko.

"Apparently it's called Yatoike Pond," I said, looking at the map. "I read somewhere they dug up most of the hills around here in search of remains. They think the whole area was once ideal for hunting down and trapping animals, because they found the remains of fences and the kinds of holes in the ground people used for catching them. I'll bet the hills around here were a pretty good place to live. I remember it said there were a couple of natural springs too," I added, drawing on the vague memory I had from reading some article.

"I'm going to live in this housing complex," said Kumiko suddenly.

"Well, the scenery's nice right now," said Amiko.

"Yes, but it's going to start looking just like the K—— apartment complex any time. Except about ten times bigger," I said.

"But it's the first time I've ever seen a view like this. I've never seen so many hills and valleys stretching away like this, as far as you can see. They look like they're shrouded in mist, those hills on the horizon. I suppose they'll eventually be developed too, and people will start living there," said Amiko.

"Hey, you see where there's still some woodland left, over there to the right? Where they're starting to build some sort of concrete structure? I'm guessing those are going to be some kind of townhouses. Now that's where I'd want to live. You'd walk out of your house into the yard and there'd be woods right in front of you. You'd be able to hear the birds singing," said Kumiko.

"The human population's never going to decrease. There are just going to be more and more of us," I said.

"Back in ancient times, life must have been hard," said Amiko, looking into the distance.

"No, you can't really say that life used to be good back then, and that it's so much worse now. I'm sure ancient civilizations had a lot of stress. There was no way of knowing when they were going to be able to capture their next meal," said Kumiko.

"What a life! It's the same worry then as now: What are we going to have for dinner tonight?" joked Amiko.

A shadow fell on Yatoike Pond, turning its surface black. We got back into the car. At my suggestion that we relax over a cup of tea, Amiko quickly found a café with a parking lot. Amiko was a considerate person. Things had never gone so smoothly with the big guy.

"I've decided. As soon as they finish that housing complex I'm going to put my name down for an apartment," Kumiko announced. "It just really appeals to me. Listen, Kyoko, Amiko. I'm definitely going to have my baby. I'm not going to marry the baby's father. He's a good man, but he's just not the daddy type. You know him, right, Amiko? He's never going to be a good father to my child. There are two types of men: ones who make good fathers and ones who don't. He never will. Right, Amiko?"

Amiko was silent. She sat there considering Kumiko as if she were afraid of answering too hastily.

I felt relief. I was glad that the big guy was not the father of Kumiko's baby after all.

"Just what is his problem?" demanded Kumiko.

"It'll be okay," replied Amiko.

"How is it going to be okay?" demanded Kumiko, suddenly turning her anger on Amiko.

"Don't be so hasty to judge him," replied Amiko.

"He's a drifter. He'll never be the kind to settle down and have a family."

The two of them slipped into a familiar, friendly style of speaking, as if they were a couple of college students again. Their exchange drifted over to me like a kind of background music that I wasn't really listening to. Their actual words had no meaning. I watched their expressions. Both women looked sometimes serious, sometimes jovial, their expressions apparently reflecting their words. If each word had been in the form of one of the sugar cubes in the bowl on our table, within seconds the table would have been buried under a mountain of words. Still, even while producing mountains of words, I guessed Kumiko was still unsure of her own thoughts—Amiko likewise. Certainly, there were many things that Amiko didn't understand. For example, maybe she would suddenly wonder why she had purchased a fifty million yen prefab house on the side of a hill for her family of four to live in domestic bliss. Maybe Kumiko would suddenly be struck by a strange feeling that having a baby, and talking of the father as an unfit parent was all nothing but some made-up story that she'd got carried away with telling. Maybe as they talked, they were both feeling helplessly trapped by the sense that the one thing they most wanted to think, the thing they truly needed to think, only existed in some other world where words were useless. And so in the end none of these thoughts was expressed in words.

Earlier, standing side by side, looking out beyond the artificially terraced land where a huge housing complex was about to be erected, looking at those hills that rolled away in the distance, each of us, separately from the others, had felt like falling to her knees and sobbing, but out of embarrassment not one of us had put that feeling into words. At least I hadn't been able to find the right words.

Buried deep in the earth, right where we'd been standing, there could well have been stone knives, stone arrowheads, stone ax-heads or broken fragments of pottery. Or perhaps the remains of a whole ancient existence lay beneath the great expanse of land laid bare before our eyes. Yet it was not that which had been so moving. It was not the view that had left me speechless—the view beyond the naked earth and waves of hill after valley lit by the fading evening light. Human beings are not that deeply affected by scenery alone. It was the realization that one day we too would become extinct and be absorbed by the landscape. There was no means of expressing that feeling in mere words.

Human beings have always sought words from other human beings, and felt secure when they heard them. But people have never really said anything. I haven't said anything myself. Well, technically, I have spoken, but it has been no more than mere phonetics.

There were hills, there were valleys, there were ponds, and there were springs, but they were simply there, a repetitive feature of the terrain, on into the distance. The land didn't send up spray like the rough waves of an ocean. These were calm and tranquil waves. For thousands, maybe tens of thousands of years, human beings had drifted in to stand, or at one time perhaps squat, on the crests of these gentle waves. There was nothing to say.

Kumiko and Amiko were laughing cheerfully.

"I've heard that there are opponents of the construction at Z——, but how can you fault modern human beings for wanting to live in the same spot that, thousands of years ago, people already thought was a great place to live?" Kumiko was saying.

"Yeah, really. Have you heard of the term *local community egoism*?" Amiko agreed. "It's really fascinating. Where I live there are eight houses. There's still a wooded area behind us. We've heard that another contractor is planning to develop that land too. As soon as they heard about it, some of our neighbors decided we should get up a petition to stop them from building there. Despite the fact that trees were torn up to build our own houses, they've now decided that no more nature should be destroyed. It's a joke."

"It was unbelievable back where I used to live. People had a petition going to try to have the area designated a "green zone" where absolutely no more apartment blocks, condos or single homes could be built. They had the attitude of, *well we're all right, we're already here* but you know they were the ones who had cut down the trees on the hillsides and built a home on any corner of any rugged crag or cliff they could find. Before they built their apartment block, their condo, or their single family home, the land was like we saw today—hills, woods, fields. *But now we're not going to let anyone else do it.* These days, anyone who dares to build a house in the area is treated like a criminal," Kumiko added.

"Rather than local community egoism, that should be known as current resident egoism," Amiko said.

"Hey, Kyoko," said Kumiko, suddenly turning her attention to me. "Kyoko! What's up with you? You're in another world. Are you sleepwalking again? Don't you think Amiko's smart? Come on Kyoko, Amiko's great, isn't she?"

"Yes, really. I'm glad you've moved into our neighborhood," I said to Amiko.

14

I heard from Yoko that Takuo had suddenly taken off for Paris. She told me that the whole trip had been financed by his parents. He hadn't discussed it beforehand with either Yoko or Tokiko; he had gone secretly to his parents to ask for their support and then upped and left, leaving behind his wife and daughter. This was no week-to-ten-day sightseeing trip—he planned to stay in Paris for a minimum of one year. The same Takuo, once seemingly abandoned to a tiny hut in the backyard, had now turned around and abandoned his wife and daughter to their cliff-top home.

"Why Paris of all places?" I asked Yoko, but I didn't think that even Takuo knew why.

"Because it's famous?" she answered detachedly, as if we were discussing a complete stranger again. "I'm going to be working full-time from now on," she added.

She'd taken a full-time position at the supermarket. Every day she put on white overalls, tied a white kerchief around her head, encased her legs in black rubber boots and worked in the water-sodden area behind the fish counter, gutting and slicing fish, doing what was traditionally men's menial labor. Even if I saw her at the supermarket, we didn't get to speak.

Yoko came over early one morning.

"Are you on your way to work?" I asked her.

"Oh, it's Veggie Club stuff . . ." she answered, but kept standing there, a vague expression on her face. Eventually she told me that she'd just heard from Katsumi's wife that a member of the Veggie Club by the name of "Kumiko" had died. Katsumi's wife had told her to come and tell Kyoko.

When Yoko left for work. I followed her out. I ran down the hill and then straight up the steep slope to the home of Kumiko's friend, Amiko. She opened the door wearing an apron.

"I'm on my way to Kumiko's apartment. Would you come with me?" I asked.

"Mama!" called the little girl from inside.

"Is something wrong?" Amiko asked.

"I think something's happened," I replied.

"I'll be right there."

I was depending on Amiko. I felt like the little girl in the house who had just cried "Mama!" A couple of minutes later Amiko came out of the house.

"What about your children?" I asked her.

"They'll be fine," replied Amiko, backing her car out of the narrow parking space. "Get in."

"Will the children really be okay?" I asked, turning to look back at the house.

"They're fine," repeated Amiko.

I waited for the car to get to the bottom of the hill before saying, "I heard Kumiko's dead."

"We don't know that for sure," she replied.

There was something reassuring about Amiko's composure.

"You know the Z—— dig site we visited the other day? Well, I just heard that the culture center is planning to display all the artifacts they dug up there. And you know the N—— apartment complex they built way north of Z—— just outside M—— City? Apparently, the site of that complex was also excavated beforehand. All the things they found there will be on display from the first of the month at the center. Since we moved here, my husband's become a big archaeology enthusiast. He's always dropping by the cultural center to pick up information about what's going on in the area," said Amiko.

"Well, next month, let's go to see it," I replied.

"I read that they found some really unusual things at the N—— apartments site. It looks as if when they were building homes they used to dig holes and put in pillars for support. The pillars were made from camphor trees, and there are still parts that haven't rotted away."

"About Kumiko . . ." I began, but Amiko continued to talk. "Apparently, there are about four hundred different archaeological dig sites in M—— City alone. There aren't a significant number of Yayoi-period remains—they're mostly from during and right around the Jomon period. Some Nara- and Heian-period stuff too, though. I've started to wonder whether my husband's interest in all the remains in this region has something to do with the fact that this is where he's going to die. Up to now, we've been continually relocating from one place to another, but now finally we've been able to settle permanently."

"You're a bit young to be deciding where you're going to die," I said.

"Well, we do have a twenty-year loan to pay off," said Amiko with a wry smile.

"What's Kumiko's boyfriend like?" I asked, but she didn't answer me.

Bizarrely, the thought that I was going to have to see my friend Kumiko dead was somehow bearable. Strange, but I didn't feel the least bit surprised by the news of Kumiko's death.

"Why didn't Kumiko marry her boyfriend? If she'd just got married none of this would have happened," I blurted out, sounding to myself like some kind of clueless parent.

"Look, we don't even know at this point that Kumiko's really dead," Amiko pointed out.

"No, I know she's dead," I replied.

"But we haven't seen her yet," insisted Amiko.

"I can really tell you're a scientist. Kumiko was the same, always insisting on the logical path."

"No, not really. I went to pharmacy school, that's all. Actually, Kumiko tended to look at things more emotionally."

"But Kumiko . . ."

"Kumiko believed in you, Kyoko," said Amiko.

"Kumiko's taken an overdose, hasn't she? That's what a pharmacist would do . . ."

Amiko was normally a very good driver, but now suddenly there was a screeching sound from the tires as she braked, and I was pitched forward in my seat.

A woman came running out of Kumiko's apartment building; maybe she'd heard the screeching tires, I'm not sure. It was Ayako. When I saw her I remembered the letter I'd gotten from Kumiko about how meeting your own self means you're about to die.

Ayako came running over. I ignored her completely and headed straight into Kumiko's apartment. Kumiko was lying on the bed, looking as if she had fallen asleep. Amiko came in right behind me.

"What about her parents?" I asked Ayako.

"I think they're on their way," she replied.

"And the police?" asked Amiko.

"I called them. They've just left," said Ayako.

I couldn't go near Kumiko. In fact, I couldn't even look at her.

"Amiko, I think I'm going to stay here a while. Why don't you go home for now? I'll call you later." I turned to Ayako. "I know you have to get to work. I'm sure you need to be getting on your way. I truly appreciate your letting me know about this. I'll wait with Kumiko until her parents get here."

"Actually, I've taken the day off," said Ayako.

"Have you? Well, Amiko, you should get back right away. Your children will be wondering where you are," I said, pretending to be accompanying Amiko outside. In truth, it was suffocating to be near my dead friend.

Just as Amiko was getting back into her car, another cream-colored car drew up next to it. The big guy was driving. I thanked Amiko and approached the man's car. On an impulse, I opened the passenger door and climbed in.

"Don't get out. Just drive," I ordered him.

It felt as if the man sitting next to me was nothing but a doll made of some kind of very strong rubber with a high elasticity. The moment I'd seen him sitting there in his car I'd mentally summoned up all my strength to throw a punch at him, but in my mind, my arm had rebounded off him ineffectually. The man looked even fatter than he had one year earlier.

"Should I drop you off at the usual place?" he asked me.

"The usual place?"

"Near your house. You're going home, right?"

"If I'd wanted to go home right now I could have gone in my friend's car."

"Ah, I see. I'm still such a dolt."

I asked him to take me up to the construction site at Z——. This time we took a different route to the truck access road and came out right above Yatoike Pond. Around here, the ground had not yet been covered with its new layer of brick-red earth; it was still the black color that had remained after the excavations. The rays of the morning sun hit the ground at an angle. Perhaps it was because I was standing at a different spot from the previous time, but the rolling waves of the hills looked completely different. This morning, in the bright sunlight, each ridge was clearly visible. The land too looked as if it had just woken up.

"So this is what they did with it," said the big guy, looking down at the flattened ground below him.

"Last Sunday I came here with Kumiko in the car of that friend you just saw. When did you last see Kumiko?" I asked him. We were standing next to each other but I couldn't look him in the face.

"I don't think I've seen her for two, maybe three months. She stopped visiting us at the apartment, but I think my wife was still meeting her," the man replied.

"So who's riding in your car with you these days?"

"No one. I'm all alone," he replied jokingly.

"So were you going to see Kumiko's body?"

"I said I'd meet my wife there."

"You were meeting your wife?" I found I had raised my voice.

"I was going to pick her up and take her to the station. Then I was going to go to work."

"Well, you'd better go then. I'll get a taxi back. I'm sorry to have taken your time."

I strode straight by the NO TRESPASSING sign and began to walk down the hillside towards Yatoike Pond. Behind me, I could hear the man's car start up. I didn't look around.

No trucks had arrived yet at the site, and there was not a soul to be seen. It occurred to me how dying meant no longer seeing anything. By dying, Kumiko had refused ever to see her child or see its father again.

Many stone tools and fragments of pottery had been unearthed here, but no human bones.

"Hey! What are you doing there?" someone yelled. There was a man down below, yelling up at me. He was wearing khaki-colored workman's pants that billowed out around his legs. Clearly, I'd been spotted and was in trouble.

Without thinking, I waved at him. I have to admit it was strange behavior to wave and run towards someone who was yelling at me.

"It's dangerous here!" he was shouting.

"I'm sorry. I'll be right down!" I called back, rushing down the hillside towards the man.

The surface of the slope was slick with water. The soles of my shoes skidded as I slid down.

"Bulldozers work in this area. It's dangerous," said the man.

I had to hold myself back from rushing up to and throwing my arms around him. It was like a cry for help, running to this man. He was around thirty, with curly hair and gentle, narrow eyes that regarded me with evident concern. This one lone man was employed to watch over this incredibly huge tract of land where they were about to build beehive-like concrete boxes to house what would probably be tens of thousands of people. When I saw him, it occurred to me that this man was the first live human being I had ever seen on this land.

"You should go back up by that road. None of the trucks come by that way in the mornings. But this road's dangerous. The big ones come this way," the man told me.

"But there's no one there yet," I argued childishly, pointing up at the road.

"Because it's too early." The man smiled.

I could lose myself in the warmth of his smiling face . . .

"It's going to be a massive complex," I remarked.

"Huge. The biggest in the region. Each block is being developed by a different company so we've got no idea of the final result."

"Are there going to be townhouses here too?"

"Hmm, I'm not sure. At least our company's not building any."

"I'd like to live in such a spacious place."

"Once construction gets underway, it'll look completely different."

"Yeah, I suppose it won't be spacious at all then."

"Right. The landscape will change completely," he said.

The landscape will change, I repeated to myself. *With Kumiko's death, the landscape has changed.*

Except the big guy. He hadn't changed at all. When I saw the big guy sitting in the car he looked so unchanged that I had automatically got into his car with him, just as if it were still last year. As I sat down beside him, I had temporarily lost track of time.

"You'd better hurry up and get out of here before the site foreman gets here and chews you out," suggested the man cheerfully.

"Don't worry, they won't catch me," I assured him as I made my way up to the road he'd pointed out to me and waved good-bye.

I couldn't help turning around and looking back at him several times, just as if I were parting from a lover. I felt as if I had fallen in love with this unknown stranger, whose path had crossed mine for just for a few moments. I felt a glow spread through my insides. A human being had suddenly emerged from the earth, and meeting him had had sent a thrill through me. There had been no one around. Why hadn't I thrown my arms around that man? I was already regretting that I hadn't. Surely the man with the curly hair, the narrow eyes, and bronzed complexion would have embraced me back? The man who knew that the landscape was about to change. He climbs the hill and I chase him up to the top. No, the opposite. He comes down into the valley to drink water. Just like beasts in the wild, we mate in full sunlight. No words. No excuses. We are swallowed up by the waves. We disappear into the landscape. Right into that giant tableau of a landscape.

15

After the dust had settled following Kumiko's suicide, Amiko called to invite me over for drinks one Saturday evening. With the kids already in bed, she said, we'd be able to talk. I had been thinking that I ought to invite Amiko over, but I never did. Kumiko had used to always complain, "Kyoko, you never let anyone into your home."

While she and I were chatting, Amiko's husband didn't show his face. It hadn't been three months since they'd moved in but already the house seemed cozy and lived-in.

"I don't think Kumiko was really pregnant after all," Amiko began.

Maybe it was because it was evening, but she had abandoned her usual neat hairstyle and her hair was loose and slightly unkempt. She had on a long skirt that covered her legs completely.

"I'm just an ordinary person," she continued. "I always believed that when you grew up you should get married, have children, and create your own family, so that's what I did. Kumiko thought differently. One time in college, she announced that she was going to shave her head and become a Buddhist nun. Her boyfriend was a doctor—a regular, ordinary guy. Just like my husband and me, the kind of person who wanted to live a normal life and raise children. He's also a brilliant doctor—the adjectives *regular* and *ordinary* only apply to his approach to life. That's the man who Kumiko decided wouldn't be a good father. I think she was projecting her own anxieties and uncertainty onto him. I don't understand Kumiko. The man who was her boyfriend didn't understand her either. She used to tease me all the time—that I was a happy homebody. My husband is a regular guy too. He thinks that having children and providing for his family is the natural thing to do. Kumiko used to look down on the everyday struggles of regular folk. Still, I was okay with that. The world's never going to change if we're all the same. I liked Kumiko. She didn't have the same values as I did, but she was a serious person. And she believed in you. Listen, Kyoko, Kumiko looked up to you. She respected you, maybe was even a little envious of you. You were married and could have had a family, but you weren't like me. So Kumiko believed in you."

She stopped speaking for a moment to add ice, whiskey, and water to my glass, then continued.

"Still, although you introduced Kumiko to the man Katsumi, she wasn't able to do what you had done. You were married, but Kumiko wasn't."

I was listening intently to Amiko's speech. A piano stood in the corner of the living room, with a metronome placed on top. That was where I was looking. A metronome imposing a monotonous beat on the sound. I supposed that right now Amiko's husband was upstairs in the children's bedroom reading them storybooks. Fairy tales by the Brothers Grimm or Hans Christian Andersen. Or perhaps *The Little Prince* or *Winnie-the-Pooh*. Or maybe traditional Japanese stories like *Earless Hoichi* or *The Grateful Crane*. Eri would kick off her covers. Her father would gently cover her up again.

"What makes you think that Kumiko wasn't really pregnant?" I asked Amiko.

"Her body shape hadn't changed at all. But I don't think it was a phantom pregnancy or anything like that. I think it was all a hoax that Kumiko dreamed up. And partly that she actually enjoyed the idea of a child for a while."

"It seems as if she couldn't work out what she wanted."

"Yes, I think the whole child thing had her in two minds. But these past couple of years she'd been trying to make a definite decision. Maybe to get rid of the doubts, she tried on the idea of a pregnancy to see how it felt. Usually, as long as it's not due to illness, there are very few people who make a categorical decision not to have children. Unless it's due to circumstances beyond their control, most people would need to have a specific ideology to make that decision. And there aren't that many people around with such a strong ideology. It's no wonder that Kumiko was so confused for so long. I think that Kumiko tried to get something from you to use to convince herself. But I think you refused to offer her the help she needed. I don't think you let her in at all."

Amiko was speaking in a low voice but her words were clear.

"I think you're right," I admitted.

I was impressed by the calm way that Amiko explained things, despite this being a direct attack on me.

"Amiko, excuse me for asking, but have you ever, inexplicably, wanted to sleep with a man besides your husband?" I asked.

"Yes, I suppose I have," she answered.

"I don't think Kumiko understood that feeling. She was always saying to me, 'You may be married, but as long as you don't have any children, you can't say you have a family.' I suppose I have to agree with that. I can't really call my domestic situation a family. I'm fundamentally different from someone who wants children but can't have them. But I've never claimed that my own way of thinking or living is the right one. It's not a question of right or wrong. I don't think of it as something to brag about or to recommend to other people. But it's something I get interrogated about. Kumiko tried to grill me about it too—time and time again. But I couldn't explain, not in a way that anyone else would understand."

Amiko's husband came in.

"Would you like some cheese?" he asked, holding out a glass plate. "I heard from Amiko that the Z—— site is massive. I'd like to go see it while it's still possible."

I was about to reply, when suddenly I was inexplicably struck by aphasia. Not a word would come out of my mouth. I was thinking of Kumiko. I couldn't stop thinking about her. How could she have considered playing for time with such a transparent lie?

"The Z—— housing complex is going to be huge," I said finally, forcing the words out with difficulty.

On a site where human beings had lived thousands of years earlier, there were once again going to be human beings. Thousands and thousands of human beings were going to gather and live on that land.

"Eri?" Amiko asked, putting on her mother's face.

"Fine," responded the father.

They were speaking in a code that was only intelligible to the two of them. Maybe Amiko saw that I'd picked up on this because she added with a laugh, "My daughter keeps hoping that our old dog might come back in the night, so it's been tough getting her to sleep."

"And the dog . . . ?"

"We got it from a neighbor. It was really cute when it was just a puppy, but of course, when it grew up it was a typical mongrel. It was so dumb we couldn't do anything with it, so when we moved here we turned it loose over on the other side of the river, assuming that it wouldn't be able to swim across. But Eri still believes it's going to come home," Amiko explained.

"With dogs they have to be a good breed or they're impossible," added Amiko's husband.

"Yeah, my own mother got rid of four mongrel kids whose father was unknown. She dumped two on her own parents, one on her older brother and the final mongrel on her cousin. I was the only one she didn't get rid of," I said.

Amiko and her husband exchanged looks. I deliberately looked away, pretending not to notice their reaction.

"What Kumiko kept asking me was whether it was my decision alone not to have children," I continued. "I think she suspected that my husband had been forced to give in to my way of thinking, and that in his heart he really wanted children. Seeing as it's always women who take the initiative when it comes to things like contraception or abortion. In fact, I think at one time Kumiko suspected that although I claimed to be married, I actually lived alone. Or at other times, she imagined that my husband and I took it in turns to play the role of child, but in the end she seemed to be frustrated by all her second-guessing, and gave up suspecting anything. I guess Kumiko was wondering whether human beings really were capable of living without children. I realize now she wanted to me to tell her straight. To narrow it down to whether I was happy or unhappy. If I had to answer in such simplistic terms, then I'd say that I'm not unhappy. I realize when I see something new that it's because I'm alive that I'm able to see it. When I see the beautiful color of the sky, it reminds me that I'm alive. Being able to make the acquaintance of you and your husband, Amiko, that's thanks to being alive.

"But most of all, I believe that the best of all would be not to have been born. We women, the ones who give birth, the creators of new life, aren't supposed to say things like that, right? Well, not only women, men aren't supposed to express things like that out loud either. But I never told Kumiko any of this. I know it's not right to speak ill of the dead but although I really liked Kumiko when she was alive, I really hate her now she's dead. It's not only Kumiko—I hate anyone who takes their own life," I said.

I regretted my words even before I'd finished speaking. Eri was standing in the kitchen in her pajamas, staring at the three adults. She didn't look at all sleepy. Rather, her pupils were wide and motionless, like a doll's eyes, as if she was trying to see something more clearly. All we could do, the three of us, was stare back at those eyes.

16

On the morning of her day off, Yoko came by to invite me to visit her cats. I felt obliged to follow her back to her house. I imagined she wanted me to see the two cats she'd been talking about before, but it turned out there were a few more than two. In fact, there were probably around ten of them, sprawled here and there around the living room.

"The family just keeps growing," said Yoko with a shy laugh.

I asked her if Tokiko kept bringing them home with her, but she shook her head and informed me with a blissful smile that they just kept turning up.

It wasn't only the number of cats, but the state of the house came as a great shock too. It was chaotic, cluttered, and dirty.

"Look—there are more out here," said Yoko, opening the back door and taking me to Takuo's former quarters, the outdoor hut. The rickety door had been left open, and the inside was crammed full of cats. I peered in, but they totally ignored me, curled up in their own personal spaces.

"Usually they're all out roaming around but they've just come back to eat. That's why I came to get you. At first, they began to gather out here in Takuo's old hut. But then there just got to be so many that they started coming indoors as well," Yoko said with pride.

"Feeding this number of animals must be hard," I said, but Yoko simply laughed in response, "Looks like I'm going out to work for the sake of the cats, doesn't it?"

I learned that she'd had a postcard from Takuo to say he'd arrived in Paris, but since then, no news at all. Tokiko was off with her boyfriend on a road trip around the island of Kyushu.

A black cat with bright green eyes began clawing at Yoko's skirt, trying to climb onto her lap. Yoko picked up a different, tiger-striped cat which had come up beside her.

"See that white one? That's the one Tokiko bought," she said, pointing.

The white cat stood out from the others. Its fur was long and fluffy. It looked almost foreign.

"Katsumi's wife says she'd like a cat too, but they're not allowed pets in the apartment. Still, it seems there are some who secretly keep them. She's fond of cats so she comes to visit sometimes. Actually, she complains that her husband doesn't like cats or dogs, so she wouldn't be able to have one of her own, whether she was in an apartment or not."

"Well, I like cats, and dogs too, but I'd never be able to keep so many," I said with a laugh.

Apparently, Ayako and Yoko had had a meeting of the minds through their mutual "hobbies" of cats and vegetables. Yoko lived close by, but my conversations with her were confined to rambling, superficial chat. We had never really had any kind of one-on-one conversation exploring anything deep. On the other hand, although we hadn't known each other for long, every time we met Kumiko and I used to talk into the night. Mostly it was joking, or sometimes mean gossip, and we knew full well that we were getting drunk and maudlin, but still we drank more, fully engaged in our conversation. Kumiko and I were similar in that neither of us really had many friends. Nor were we at ease chatting away in a whole crowd of people. We were each seeking a partner. A partner for linguistic communication. We both enjoyed that moment when, in the middle of joking around with a conversation partner, you suddenly sense you've touched on something deeper.

"So how's the veggie thing going?" I asked Yoko.

"I'm still doing it. Lately I've been going to the farm once a month with Katsumi's wife."

Cats stretched out on floor cushions, cats hiding in cardboard boxes, cats curled up on chairs, cats on all fours, their tongues lapping at plates of food, on the sofa, on the stairs, stuck to Yoko, in the kitchen batting at a dangling apron string; everywhere the animal smell was overwhelming.

When I'd finally reached the top of the ridge and looked down, the man who'd appeared at the Z—— construction site had vanished again, right behind the little patch of woods where Kumiko had wanted to live. The black earth was the loamy layer of the Kanto Plain that had been dug up. I'd seen the term "Tachikawa Loam" in a pamphlet. It seems all the red earth was brought in by truck. The red was used like a kind of layer of fabric lain on top of the black loam.

"I heard that Kumiko's parents took her body away with them that day," said Yoko.

"Right, they didn't let anyone get close. It seems they were from rural Gunma Prefecture. They just loaded everything up in their car and left. I suppose the funeral was there too. By the evening there was absolutely nothing left. Kumiko was completely gone."

I staggered down the cliff from Yoko's house. I skidded several times, and ended up with dirt in my shoes. I felt as insecure as a little toddler. My eyes were wide open just as Eri's had been that night. In one eye, I could see Kumiko standing on that black earth, the hills and valleys stretching in waves into the distance; in the other I could see the face of the curly-haired man. The two images dissolved, turned to liquid and began to pour from my eyes.

I arrived at the train station and got into a taxi. I wiped away the liquid images with the back of my hand.

"Don't forget!" I was screaming inside. I didn't know whether I was screaming at the big guy, at Kumiko, at Kumiko's parents, or at something or someone vague and indistinct. But what did I mean by "Don't forget"?

"Would you follow the directions as I give them to you? I know the way very well," I told the taxi driver.

I remembered Kumiko's words. "You may be married, Kyoko, but you're still alone." Kumiko was always saying that.

No, I'm not alone. Well, sort of, but not really . . . You know, maybe she was right.

Kumiko had been afraid. "Hey, Kyoko. How can you bear it? How can you stand being alone?" she had once asked me.

Giant trucks were rolling in, loaded up with sections of giant walls. I guessed they were carrying chunks of prefab buildings, churned out in some factory.

"If one of those fell on you you'd be crushed flat," said the taxi driver.

I could see people in the area of brush on the way. They wore rubber boots and had tool belts around their waists.

"Excuse me, Ma'am, you realize there'll be no taxis to bring you back. Would you like me to wait?" asked the driver.

"It's fine. You can go," I answered.

Like the last time, I descended the hill towards Yatoike Pond. In the distance, I could just about make out what looked like an empty concrete box stuck on top of the red earth. From where I stood, the doorway and windows were just tiny holes. I set out to circle the pond, staying within the wooded area. On a distant hill, I could see the red roofs of several dozen homes already inhabited. They looked like a line of dolls' houses. Way, way over there. There were so many hills in this black earth.

Surveying equipment had been set up in the woods and I could see two or three men peering through it into the distance.

"The tank road along that ridge over there . . . " I heard one of them say.

The term "tank road" was a relatively recent one, probably coined during the war. Apparently, these days it was being used to mean an access road for construction trucks.

I stood there in a trance for a moment, then began to run down the slope of the woods.

I heard a horn sound a few times from the construction road above me. I was wearing a yellow shirt, so I must have been clearly visible from up there. I was already in the restricted area. There was a gate to the access road up on the ridge, with a guard standing watch. However, on the day of Kumiko's death, the big guy's car had come up the steep road from the already-inhabited valley on the far side, away from that gate, and I had told the taxi driver to come the same way.

"Hey, it's dangerous!" yelled some guy in a hard hat from the window of a mud-splattered truck. Then, "What? Not you again!"

The truck bed was empty, and the truck was parked diagonally across the narrow road that led up from the red earth. The road looked white in contrast. There were hills and valleys all over in this red earth, this black earth—you'd never know when a truck might suddenly pop up. It really was no safe place for pedestrians to be.

"This is the most dangerous spot right here. There are trucks going in and out all the time," said the man in the hard hat. I finally realized that it was the very same curly-haired man who had so abruptly appeared from, and then abruptly vanished into, the earth that day.

"I'm sorry. I'll get out of here right away," I said, automatically bowing my head in apology.

"If you take that road they'll stop you because you obviously don't belong here," said the man.

"Then would you give me a ride back?" I asked him.

I climbed up into the passenger seat. His truck passed through the gate, descended the steep slope and passed through the maze of ups and downs of the residential neighborhoods. We emerged onto the main highway.

"I'll get out here. Thank you for your trouble," I said.

"I can take you to the station if you want. It's on my way," said the man, taking off his helmet. "What were you doing there? You were lucky—a week later, and it could have been fatal. All the other construction companies are arriving this week. For the moment it's still only us and one or two others."

By the gate, I'd seen a large signboard with a plan of the whole construction site. As he'd said, the site was divided up into more than twenty different sections, each with its own number and the name of a construction company.

"Honestly, I came today because I was hoping to see you again," I said with a smile.

"Look, it's no joke. The place I worked before, a steel beam slid off a truck bed and seriously injured a little boy. There are no traffic signals in a place like that. Especially this one I'm working now—whichever way you enter the site, the roads are all on a steep slope. It's really dangerous," he said as if trying to make a small child understand.

"I mean it. That last time, I turned around when I got to the top of the slope and you'd vanished. I thought if I came back I might get to see you again."

He didn't reply, but I saw that he was embarrassed.

"I know you think I'm teasing you, but I'm not. It's the truth," I insisted.

"I can't believe a woman would come alone to a place like that," he said.

"A friend of mine asked me to go and see it with her because she was thinking of renting a place there. It was about a month back. Then my friend died suddenly, and I came back by myself. And that was when you yelled at me . . ."

"You know most of those apartments are going to be for sale."

"Are you going back to work?" I asked.

"Yeah."

"I'll be back again, then."

"I don't advise it."

"There's no law against viewing the scenery, is there?"

"There'll be bulldozers."

"I know you still think I'm lying to you, but I really did want to see you again. And then when I really did run into you it was quite a surprise. I'd like to meet you one more time—in those woods above the pond. I'll be waiting there."

The truck picked up speed on the national highway. I had no idea where we were heading. The seats were higher up than in a regular car and I had the sensation of looking down on everything from a great height. Then suddenly, we were on the expressway. Where was I going? Who was this stranger driving me, and where was he from? I didn't care about Kumiko any more. In death, Kumiko's face was a pale, moss color. Her mouth seemed to be pouting. Kumiko's parents had just neatly cleaned everything up as if the whole business of Kumiko's death could be resolved with money. Just as if Kumiko were something dirty that had to be disposed of as soon as possible. Still, I have to admit that technically a dead body is something dirty. Because it putrefies by the second. If you leave it lying around for a couple of days the smell is enough to make people want to throw up . . .

That black earth was also made from the bodies of decayed human beings. It's possible that what the Japanese call *chirei*, or earth spirits, are really clusterings of the souls of decayed human beings. Those clusters were now being torn apart by bulldozers. This man would be transporting fragments of crushed souls in the back of his truck.

"You know, that time I was on my way to take a leak when I saw you and hollered," said the man with a dry laugh. His voice bounced around me pleasantly. I began to feel my spirits lift again.

"Now that sounds interesting. Next time I'm going to watch. I'm going to hide in the woods," I told him, making him laugh out loud.

Chatting with this man put me in such a lighthearted mood that I felt as if I could go on forever.

"If you're not careful, I really will come and watch," I warned him.

"You've got a dirty mind," he laughed. "Look out! What a jerk!" he yelled, apparently at a car that had pulled out suddenly.

"I guess you shouldn't mess with trucks. They're the bosses of the road," I remarked.

"You're right about that," he said.

"This is just like the movies!"

"It's not as fun as it looks in the movies," he replied.

"Then let's make it fun," I suggested.

17

"If you head north from the T——housing complex the land is still untouched. It feels as if you're in some remote mountainous area. There are a few thatched-roof cottages here and there but they're mostly uninhabited. A friend of mine heard about them and decided she wanted to rent one, so I took her up to see the area. The rent was really cheap—they only wanted ten thousand yen a year. And because they're made the old way, the houses are really spacious. It's the mother of one of Tokiko's friends. She rented the house up there to weave cloth. Could you do me a favor and buy something?" said Yoko, ever the old woman.

I supposed Yoko just genuinely liked to help people out, as she was always asking a favor on behalf of someone or other.

"If it were me I'd be pretty scared up there in a house all by myself. She dyes all her yarn herself too—she uses all-natural plant dyes. Her daughter—the one who's Tokiko's friend—recently quit junior college and moved to the Kansai area. She's not married or anything, but I think she's gone with some man. Just a table centerpiece or something small, but please buy something from her."

Yoko seemed to have extended her range of ways to help others out since Takuo left for Paris. I too had received a postcard from Takuo, written in a trembling, practically illegible hand: *It doesn't matter where you go—it's all the same. I've decided to die here.*

Yoko took me by bus via the T—— housing complex to visit the thatched-roof houses. I accepted her invitation to go as if she'd invited me to ride a boat on the pond in the middle of some park. The T—— housing complex felt about the distance away of the opposite side of a pond. I'd gone on the pond at D—— Park with the big guy, and monster-sized koi carp would stick their open mouths above the surface of the murky water, gulping at the air. Although their bodies looked sluggish, coated with a thick, opaque layer the color of mud, their mouths snapped eagerly. I'd wondered aloud if these koi had been living there for five hundred years, but the big guy had offered no reply. Those fish were real monsters.

"It sure is a walk from the bus stop," said Yoko. It was true that it had been a fair distance, and all on a winding mountain trail through forest, so it had seemed a real hike.

The house itself was hidden in a small valley. Inside, there was a loom and other weaving tools set on the gleaming black wooden floor. The floor was cut away in the center for a traditional sunken *irori* cooking hearth. Dressed in traditional cotton work pants, and kneeling directly on the wooden floorboards without so much as a cushion, was the mistress of the house, Misawa-san.

"You know, I do have electricity, gas, and running water," she said with a laugh.

"But you don't have a phone, do you?" asked Yoko.

"No, and that's a blessing," Misawa replied.

"It must be nice that no one bothers you," I said.

"Right. It's ideal for working. Still, after you haven't spoken to anyone for more than three days, it starts to feel a little surreal. I always end up talking to myself."

Misawa was busy spreading her work out on the floor as she spoke. Each piece was composed of subtle gradations of faint colors, just like an evening sky.

"They're not very fancy, I'm afraid," offered Misawa, humbly. "The coloring is a little too transparent. These pieces are a bit uninteresting, they remind me of a mountain hermit's. No one wants something that looks like a robe woven by a mountain hermit," she continued, self-effacingly. Admittedly, the pieces were all rather pale.

"The colors are beautiful," said Yoko. Her flattery was simple and sincere.

"Yes, it's mostly women who buy these kinds of pieces. My work doesn't really appeal to masculine tastes," said Misawa.

"That's because you're living closeted away up here," said Yoko.

"So are you deliberately estranging yourself from other people here?" I asked.

"Yes," replied Misawa firmly.

"On the other hand, if a man came up to visit you here, no one would know," I pointed out.

"Right," she said in the same firm manner.

"The other day I spent about an hour with a brown-skinned man who mysteriously appeared from the Jomon-era remains at Z——," I said.

"I believe you're married, aren't you?" asked Misawa.

"Yes, I am."

"When you're married it becomes very difficult for either men or women to have friends of the opposite sex. I'm quite envious of you. I'd really like to have male friends too, but men always seem to end up being lovers or husbands, and never just friends. When women spend all their time with other women they become somehow warped."

"Oh no, I'm so sorry that you've had to put up with two more women," I said, and the three of us laughed. "He took me for a drive in his truck and I had a really good time. You know, I really do tell my husband about all my good times," I assured them.

"Now that is just wrong. That makes you partners in crime," teased Misawa.

I bought one of the sunset-colored fabrics, mainly because I'd taken a liking to this person called Misawa.

"Did you know that they've found the remains of cave dwellings in the hillside on the far side of that T—— housing complex near here? And M——City has the greatest concentration of pre-Jomon remains that anyone has ever found. They hadn't even developed weaving techniques back then. I suppose they used to wear animal hides," I said.

"At night it's pitch-black here in the mountains. Sometimes I hear voices—I'm sure they're not animal sounds. I'm not sure what they are. Definitely not cats. I'm convinced they're human. But my nearest neighbor lives over the next mountain. It must come all the way from there. The woman who lives there makes dolls. A professional doll maker. Her real name is something very unusual. It's said that her family has been well-known for generations for being in the cremation business," said Misawa.

"I once bought one of her dolls. She's very famous," Yoko added. "When Tokiko's leg was injured in a car accident around the time Takuo went away, I got a postcard from her promising to repair the doll. When I pulled it out from the back of the closet, I found one of its legs had been broken off."

"If she tells me that a man's coming to visit, one always turns up the very next day. Yoko here thinks it's creepy but it doesn't bother me. Her dolls aren't exactly what you'd call cute, but she's a friendly soul. The dolls are modeled on those straw figures that people use to take revenge on someone. Interesting isn't it that the word *doll* in Japanese is written with the characters meaning *human form*? And kind of disturbing too, when you think about it."

"I suppose it's possible that the noise from my loom might echo eerily over at her place too. And the voices of my male customers or my own voice might sound sinister to her. Like the cries of some wild beast. Over in the T—— housing complex there are so many concrete nesting boxes just teeming with people—there must be plenty of them making wild-animal noises there too. Or maybe they're practicing self-control, not to sound like wild beasts. Whenever I talk to Yoko about the voices from over the next mountain, she always claims it's the voices of the dolls I can hear and gets all scared. But I know they're human voices, those strange sounds. Whenever a man comes to visit, she makes animal noises, the doll maker. You know, it's becoming more like a village of animals around here all the time," said Misawa with a laugh.

Misawa invited me to take a walk. What she called "the next mountain" turned out to be a gently sloping wooded trail.

"It must be nice to live with your husband, just the two of you," said Misawa as we strolled through the woods.

"I've never really stopped to think about whether it was nice or not," I replied.

"And that's good," said Misawa.

"Without children we've been like an old married couple from the outset. We've never been so focused on all the hard work and pleasures of raising kids that we suddenly turned around one day and realized we'd grown old. No, we were aware of the aging process from the start. We've been able to enjoy that slowly."

"I envy you. At the age of fifty I've decided that I'd like to live that way, but partners like that don't just appear out of nowhere," said Misawa.

"You know, you say you envy me, but it's not all smooth sailing. My husband and I do have to struggle to make it work."

"Well, I realize that. But it must be fun anyway."

"Well, now that you mention it, I suppose it is fun."

"Please come and visit me again. And bring your husband next time."

I glanced at Misawa's face, and for a moment, her grin reminded me of a rather cute and cuddly wild animal.

18

My spirits were lifted every time I thought about the man who gave me a ride in his truck. I could hear the sound of waves inside me. As the wind grew stronger, the waves gradually built up higher and higher, soaring into the sky before finally crashing to the shore and spreading throughout my whole body. The curved contours of this huge soaring wall of water rose to envelop the very sky, hung there, then in the blink of an eye came crashing down to the sand. Within this soaring wall of a wave was an alternate universe of pure nothingness. The wave's inner wall, its mucous membrane.

The wave crashes. Water that stood rigid as steel is, in a fleeting moment, smashed to millions of pieces.

The curly-haired man had appeared before me without warning, as if flung out from the crest of one of the waves that formed this land, but I had subsequently tossed him from my own wave. I had chosen not to become involved with this man, not to push my wave to even greater heights.

My evil intent had reared its ugly head before I ever climbed into that truck. In the presence of that vast expanse of black earth, stripped of its natural surface layer, I had been close to stripping away my own surface, and opening myself up completely. In the distance, far beyond the expanse of black earth, the waves of hills and valleys seemed to vanish into a faint, whitish haze. The spray from my own wave danced on their distant plains.

The man with the shiny brown skin nonchalantly urinated in the wood and drove a truck.

I had sat beside him in that truck and offered myself to him sexually, but then abruptly cut him off. In that moment, as I opened myself up completely, I had no longer felt like a woman, but like a man. Or rather, I felt as if both woman and man lived within me. The sexual act between me and the man sitting by me at the wheel stayed entirely within my head. But at that moment (and this didn't feel like some sort of deluded dream within my head) my whole being had turned to fluid inside a bag made of skin. I had a sense that this sac that contained my whole self was on the point of bursting and spraying out the fluid of my self. The water would swell until eventually it flooded the whole truck. At that point the man I called my husband would appear. And I, not my husband, would kick the man with the shiny brown skin out of the truck. The man who was my husband would know that I was fluid inside a sac shaped like a human being, and, ladle in hand, would scoop up the water that poured from the truck.

"It's a lie that when you die there's nothing left of you but bones. Your body dissolves away until it's nothing but water and then you disappear," I would say to the man who was my husband. This was because I had studied the vast black land far too much. I recalled how much I had wanted to take the curly-haired man with the shiny brown skin who had appeared from the black earth, and have sex with him right there on the ground until I turned to water and vanished into the earth. It had to be right there in that place. The moment we'd climbed into the truck, it was already too late. As my body decomposed in the black earth, my water would soak into the ground and enter a world deep, deep down. I'd enter that world never to emerge again. An inverted version of the world above, it would consist of a great sterile vacuum where nothing propagated or grew. It would be filled with a mist formed by droplets of water from all the ancient peoples who had already dissolved. These water droplets would never form waves or rise up.

Kumiko is running towards me. No, it's Amiko. The blinding sun is right behind her as she runs, so it's hard to see her face. Now I can see the sweat rolling down her wide forehead, in gleaming golden drops.

"I needed some exercise so I've started running," Amiko announced.

"This is a good area to work out, with all the hills," I replied. Amiko nodded, trying to catch her breath.

"Do you mind if I come in for a moment?" she asked, letting herself into the front yard of my house.

I had been burning trash, but now I poured water on the fire to put it out.

"I know we haven't known each other very long, and this might sound a bit strange, but I've got a bit of a problem," said Amiko, standing by the smoldering fire. She was wearing dark blue jogging pants, tight at the ankles.

"It seems my husband is having an affair. I guess it's not really that surprising, since he's a man. Even I might have an affair someday, I suppose, so that in itself is fine. The problem is the children. My daughter's reaction has been so intense it's scary."

Clouds float in the sky like smoke or mist; if you take your eye off them for an instant they vanish completely, scattered by the wind. Listening to Amiko's words, I felt as if I was watching those clouds.

"So then I decided to have my mother take care of the children for a while. So what does my husband do? He decides not to keep it a secret at all. He's having his affair full-out in the open. Unbelievable!"

I was practically in another world.

"Would you like to come in for some tea?" I asked.

"No thanks. I'm in the middle of my run," replied Amiko, heading back to the gate.

That's fine. Do as you like, I thought.

Yoko had also dropped by a couple of days earlier and rambled on about this and that. Takuo's mother had fallen critically ill, and a telegram had been sent to Takuo in Paris. He'd returned to Japan, but couldn't even be bothered to speak to his wife and daughter at the airport. Instead, he'd headed straight back to his parents' home in floods of tears. By the time Takuo had arrived his mother was already dead.

"He cried all the way home on the plane," Yoko told me. Her tone was completely devoid of criticism or any suggestion of her making fun of Takuo. It wasn't exactly an everyday occurrence for a forty-year-old man with a wife and child, who receives a telegram informing him of his mother's critical condition, to react by crying all the way to the airport and onto a plane; to continue sobbing for the duration of his international flight, then on his arrival back in Japan to rush immediately to his mother's home, weeping uncontrollably all the way. Yoko didn't seem to find anything strange in her husband's behavior.

Nor did Amiko seem to find her husband's involvement in a passionate love affair anything out of the ordinary. Amiko differed from Yoko in that she preferred to consider her husband's situation logically. In this case she used the perfectly valid logic—that, as her husband was a man, he was quite likely to have an affair. This same affair had plainly shaken up the whole family—she'd already taken her kids to stay with their grandparents—but she was hiding her anxiety behind cold logic. It might just have been Amiko's pride, I supposed. When we'd stopped off for a cup of tea on the way home from Z—— with Kumiko, Amiko had said, "I hate the concept that a husband's unfaithfulness, or occasionally a wife's, is what keeps a marriage strong. It's true that sex isn't a problem, but you can't stop someone falling in love. Then there's nothing that can be done." I had wondered then whether Amiko was prepared for the fact that if either she or her husband had a love affair, the family living in that pretty, white, fifty-million-yen house would be torn apart.

If you had happened to pass by the eight homes that included Amiko's before anyone had moved in, you would have seen what appeared to be a showcase of construction companies' model homes, each one different from the next. There had still been a few trees left standing on the hillside where Amiko's house had been built, but now there was one spot where all the remaining trees had been cut down. Here, according to Amiko, instead of prefab houses, they were about to build some monstrous, mansion-sized homes.

Even in the residential areas where people had been living for years, that hillside land had been sold off in pieces, each purchaser custom-ordering his house, so that walking through the area often felt like strolling through a model home exhibition. I imagined these homeowners had collected pamphlets from various housing construction companies, or perhaps scoured housing architecture magazines, in the attempt to build themselves a good-looking home on a low budget. As you strolled down any street, you could see the results of all their efforts, displayed in what had now become a brand-new residential neighborhood. There were prefab homes, faux Spanish style, faux American colonial style, but really they were pretty much all the same.

Wherever you go there are hills, wherever you go there is at least one steep flight of steps, and if you climb up to what was once the road along the ridge, all of a sudden, for the first time ever, the other side of the hill comes into view. Occasionally you stumble upon an unexpected glimpse of a tall department store in downtown M——City.

In the early 1930s, when the first private railway company began operating in M—— City, the number of passengers using T—— Station, the one regularly used by Yoko, Amiko and myself, was two hundred annually. Thirty years later, M—— City's population had risen to sixty thousand people. But now, fifty years later, that number had shot up to three hundred thousand. This rapid increase was mostly due to the apartment complexes. These gently rolling hills and valleys, five hundred feet above sea level, attracted human beings at a ferocious pace. People paired up, had families, and came to settle here.

In the house where once there was a family of four, Amiko was now living alone.

Normally unemotional, Amiko had become depressed. This had seemed pretty clear when she'd called me to say that she'd baked a cake and I should come over, which she'd phrased more like an order than a request. It was no problem for me to drop by on my way home from the market. Although it was still only three in the afternoon, I found Amiko with all the curtains drawn and a glass of brandy in her hand.

"I'd be lying if I said I didn't feel totally miserable," she said. "You know, it's already been ten years since I met my husband, so you'd think it wouldn't be particularly surprising that he's having an affair. It's perfectly natural for his interest and curiosity to turn to some other person or thing. I mean, that's just human nature. But if I decide to accept this situation now, my family will be destroyed. I know it sounds strange, but I totally understand the way my husband feels right now. He never started calling me 'Mama' along with the kids. That's the kind of person he is. He's always called me by my name. He has never taken my identity as a wife or as a woman, bundled them together and turned them into one single identity, a mother. He hates the idea of his home turning into a single-mother household where the man acts like one of the kids, calling his own wife 'Mama' or 'Mother.' And that's the kind of person I admire, both as a man and as my husband. I completely understand that it's not because he fell out of love with me that he started an affair. But it's still painful. I have no idea whether this is some kind of sudden, intense passion that is going to fizzle out anytime now, or whether it's going to get more serious as time goes on. It'd be just as painful if it were the other way around and I were the one having the affair."

"I don't believe a couple with children should ever split up. I'm against it. For any reason whatsoever, I'm completely against it." Shocked by my own vehemence, I tried to cover it up with a laugh.

Amiko stared at me in amazement.

"I'm a hundred percent opposed. A couple who came together for love, had children together for love, whatever may come between them, there is absolutely no way they should separate," I repeated.

"You can't mean absolutely no way?" said Amiko, giggling.

"Absolutely no way," I giggled back.

"So it's really absolutely no way, then?" she giggled again.

"I know you think I'm old-fashioned, but the two of you decided to have children. I don't know if it's a serious affair or what, but it's too much for kids to bear when their parents argue about that kind of thing. It's so selfish. Even though I'm not particularly fond of children, I'm not a parent myself, so I'm always going to put myself in the place of a child and feel a child's outrage. Parents are selfish."

"So you're saying that I should be like the women of my mother and grandmother's generations and put up with anything and everything purely for the sake of the children?"

"No, that's not what I'm saying. I'm saying that a man and a woman decided they liked each other, loved each other, became passionate, and fell into bed together. They got married with the fantasy of creating a family. And children were an essential requirement for the making of that family. And so they had children, and those children were very cute. The man and the woman would say things like 'Oh she looks just like you,' or 'Doesn't he look a lot like me?' 'Oh look, he just smiled!' 'She stood up by herself'; 'Oh no, he just pooped.' It was all so much fun. But then they couldn't just die satisfied, they still had to obsess over whether or not to have an affair. And then the worst-case scenario became reality: they simply forgot about their children and lived entirely for themselves. See—selfish."

"Wow. Well there's a counterattack I wasn't expecting," said Amiko with a laugh.

"Well you know what they say: your closest ally is also your enemy."

"But you know what, thank you so much for listening. I really feel better having got it off my chest," said Amiko, getting up and opening the curtains.

"People have children, those children grow up and the parents die. It'd be simple if that was all there was to it. But life is long, and it can be painful," I said.

"So true," replied Amiko, but this time she wasn't laughing.

If Kumiko had been here with us, I wonder what she would have said. Kumiko had been planning to keep a child away from its father.

"I wonder what would happen if I had an affair?" mused Amiko, a far-off look in her eyes.

"I guess if it was a love strong enough to make you leave your husband, then you'd probably end up abandoning up your children too."

"You may be right. I'd be completely out of control."

"You're still only in your thirties. And things don't change when you reach your forties. Sometimes there's a feeling in your belly, as if you want to destroy everything by having an affair. It comes wriggling to the surface like a mosquito larva that you can't control," I said.

"Like a mosquito larva?"

"A mosquito larva . . . Hmm, maybe that wasn't the best analogy," I acknowledged.

This time Amiko's laugh was sunny again.

I left Amiko's house and set off to walk home. The lights were on in all the houses on the hillside. Beneath each light was a dining table, and I imagined parents and children gathered together around each one.

19

I got back from a ten-day trip to the Kansai region to find a letter from Yoko pushed through the front door. She wrote that, following the death of Takuo's mother, she had been called on to take care of Takuo's widowed father, and was moving immediately into his home in Shizuoka prefecture. The Hibiya household had left the land of rolling hills and valleys. She wrote that the house on the cliff was up for sale. I went the next day to check it out and there it was, standing empty, a realtor's "For Sale" sign in the front yard. Yoko had written that she wanted to leave me a memento and that she would ask Misawa to pass it on to me.

I didn't know what his family's occupation was, but I assumed that Takuo came from a wealthy background. Yoko would probably no longer have to work in a supermarket. And Tokiko would doubtless become the heartthrob of all the local youths. I pictured grandfather, parents, and granddaughter all sitting around the dinner table. Yoko was a great cook. I knew because every year she would carefully pickle plums, shallots, whatever vegetable was in season. She'd also produce unusual varieties of jam, and often brought me gifts of whatever she'd been making. I was sure that Takuo's father would be equally delighted with everything she made.

When I went to call on Misawa, there was a man at her cottage. Of course, as she had no phone I was obliged to drop by unannounced. In spite of my repeated apologies, Misawa assured me it was no problem.

The man was dressed in a heavy sweater. On both front and back there was a great bird with outspread wings. I'd read a magazine article about sweaters like this. They were knitted and worn by a native North American tribe that lived on an island in southern Canada. The bird with the open wings was the mythological thunderbird. According to this tribe's legend, there had lived a giant orca which had been devouring almost to extinction the local population of salmon, a staple of the tribe's diet. A thunderbird had come to their aid, fought this orca, and won. To honor this thunderbird, the tribe had made it a recurring symbol in their arts and crafts.

The man went out back without uttering a word.

"I've got a bad reputation as a slave driver whenever I've got a man around to do odd jobs," said Misawa.

There were several thick logs burning in the *irori* hearth.

"It doesn't matter how long I keep the kerosene heater on, it doesn't warm this place. This kind of house was meant to be heated by a log fire. I've sent him out back to collect wood."

She placed a paper bag in front of me.

"This is what Yoko left for you. It's the doll we talked about when you both came. I think it's an important memory from

Yoko's youth. She saw it at a doll exhibition and was immediately drawn to it. It was just a coincidence that it turned out to have been made by the doll maker who lives near here. Yoko must have had wealthy parents. Even thirty years ago that doll maker's dolls weren't cheap." Misawa was clearly trying to convince me to look inside the bag, but I left it where it was.

I stared at the little balls of lint scattered here and there on the floor.

"Do you have a *yoki*?" came the man's voice from the back door.

"Huh? What's a *yoki*?" asked Misawa.

"A kind of ax. In the Kansai region they call that hatchet thing you use for chopping wood a *yoki*," I told her.

"Oh, is that what it's called?" said Misawa. Then in a louder voice, directed out back, "I've only got a saw, I'm afraid!"

"It's like a scene from a traditional Japanese fairy tale around here," I said with a laugh.

"It really is. Around here, nothing gets done without the requisite old man." Again, she raised her voice for the man to hear, "Umino-san! Would you like a cup of tea?" There was no response. She turned back to me. "I don't think a cup of tea will do it for him. He prefers sake, day or night."

A sound came from the kitchen.

"Go ahead and help yourself to the sake," Misawa called to him. "Without a drop of sake in that man you'd never get a word out of him," she continued, more to herself than to anyone else.

The man in the thunderbird sweater seemed younger than Misawa, but perhaps that was because of the sweater. He must have been around fifty, too.

"About the doll, if it really isn't to your taste, I'll return it to its mother in the woods," Misawa offered, right as I was leaving.

"No, Yoko made the effort to leave it for me, so I'll take it," I said, picking up the bag and setting off down the mountain path.

I'd heard that in China, the phrase "to make a doll" was synonymous with starting something evil. Long ago, they used to bury a straw doll in a grave along with a dead body. Over time, the custom was modified and the straw doll became a life-sized wooden doll, known as a tomb figure. Eventually, because these figures looked so lifelike, a new custom came into being where a second person would give up their life in order to be buried alongside their master—a servant literally following his master to the grave. It wasn't the case that burying a second human being alongside a corpse was so terrible an act that they substituted a doll for the person. It happened the other way around—because the doll resembled a flesh and blood person, this gave someone the idea of using a real live human being. At first glance, this story feels like the reverse of normal human behavior, but in reality it is more likely that a doll would remind you of a human being, rather than a human being remind you of a doll. And this is how it came to be that, rather than a doll being used as a sacrifice in place of a human being, a human being was actually sacrificed in place of a doll.

The doll that Yoko had given me was a young girl with black hair, wearing a hat. She had on a pair of beautifully stitched shoes, made of real leather. Under her green velvet dress, the high-quality lace of her petticoats had been torn in places, but this doll had clearly not been made by some amateur doll maker. The work was intricate and it certainly must have been a costly purchase. If the family of that doll maker had really lived deep in the valley behind the T—— housing complex since ancient times, as Misawa had told me; if their original occupation had been the cremation of corpses, and here was their descendant—a doll maker—then it was easy to imagine them having long ago made dolls to bury with the dead. But the story was too good to be true.

I sat Yoko's doll on the shelf with my other dolls, souvenirs of all my trips to the provinces, and was sure that they'd all get on fine together.

20

The woods and open spaces that I used to pass when I was out walking were gone, and here and there new houses were under construction. In the middle of the residential zone, there was a wide open space like a schoolyard where there had stood four ginkgo trees, each probably several hundred years old, and a giant plane tree so thick that it would take two people, arms completely outstretched, to circle its trunk. Chainsaws had whittled them away from the tops downwards, until finally they'd been uprooted completely. I picked up a supple branch that had been severed from the very top of the plane tree, several spiky seed balls still attached, and brought it home to hang on my veranda. I'm not sure why, but that open land also had a well in it. Work had begun on twelve new houses in that space.

A little further along, there had been a small copse of deciduous trees. Only in winter when their leaves had fallen could you stand at the top of the slope and see the rows of houses in the next valley. But now most of the trees were gone and a large concrete building resembling a European castle had appeared. There had also been rows of pines on the south-facing slope of the ridge road, but now many large trees were missing. Piles of massive rocks had appeared along the side of the road, as if someone was planning to build a great lookout tower or something. Wherever there was space, people would come.

The prefab homes in such-and-such neighborhood had long been finished, and the gossip had been that they were all forty million yen, so who was going to pay that, who would live in such an expensive place? Yet a mere two years later, those houses seemed a bargain compared to the new prefab homes built by X Construction Company on another plateau in another neighborhood. Rumor had it those houses were going for sixty million apiece.

There were some big houses by the station in prime locations on the top of the hill, each with plenty of land for a garden. Their occupants had settled here thirty or forty years ago when the land had been cheap thanks to its remote location. Now newcomers looked up at the generously sized plots with their mature trees, and sighed with envy. If there was a single space in the rows of these houses, a gap in the row of teeth, the empty land would be divided into four separate plots and four more houses would be built. Those newcomers in turn, with total disregard for the atmosphere created by the meticulously kept trees and plants of their neighbors in the older homes, would use their tiny yards that faced the street to hang pants, shirts, and sheets. In turn, this behavior drew the contempt of the earlier settlers.

Elderly white-haired couples could be seen emerging from the thirty- or forty-year-old homes and silently shuffling off down the street for a walk, or else burning leaves in their yard. At most of these old homes, a portion of the lovingly tended garden or stone wall had been sacrificed to make room for a garage, and middle-aged couples would emerge in their cars and set off down the street. These were the children who had been born and raised in those same houses, but were now grown up. It was necessary for them to knock down the stone walls to build their garages. The newer houses, whether they were situated at the top of a cliff, or halfway up a steep slope, had garages already attached. Twenty-some years ago, the older people would say how much trouble it was to get to the train station on a rainy day, how they would slide around in the mud in their rubber boots. These days, rainy days brought lines of people waiting at the station for a taxi home. Even if it wasn't raining, there were people who took a taxi rather than walk the ten minutes or so home, so the lines never did get any shorter.

I was used to walking everywhere, but from time to time Amiko would offer me a ride. And so it was that lately, if I had too much to carry or I was going to one of the major supermarkets, or even to D——Park, I had started to get into the habit of going by car instead. Still, unlike the big guy from the K——apartment complex, Amiko never had so much spare time that she got in the car just to "drive around." Amiko's children had long since returned home, followed in quick order by her husband, and I had never spoken to her on the subject again.

Amiko's husband was what was known as an elite salaryman, or fast-track professional, so regardless of the twenty-year loan they'd taken out, they still made a steady living. Amiko had recently started to take classes at a language school. When she was a kid, her father had been temporarily assigned to a post in Germany, so perhaps it was German she was studying. It seemed she was planning to start her own career within the next few years.

"Obviously in the days when men went out hunting it made sense for the women to stay at home and take care of the children, but it doesn't make sense to allocate jobs in the computer age as if it were still the Stone Age. I'm not saying that women can't be proud of themselves unless they make their own money. I just feel that the old-fashioned division of gender roles doesn't work anymore. We're not living in some ancient era of agriculture when everyone had to be involved in the cultivation of the rice. All those traditional roles just don't make sense today. I believe it's all about to change," she told me.

Amiko was bright and intelligent, and her vitality reminded me that a woman's true beauty peaks in her mid-thirties. It was hard to believe that those days of sitting behind closed curtains drinking brandy from morning to night had ever existed. Looking at this new Amiko I couldn't help seeing Kumiko again. The Kumiko who stood stiff with anger upon the hilltop in Z—— and glared out over the spreading waves of hills and valleys. What if Kumiko had looked at me and had the illusion that she was looking at her own self? This was the same person who had been so unnerved by the phrase, "If you ever meet yourself in real life, then you're about to die." Kumiko didn't look like Ayako. She couldn't possibly have seen herself in Ayako . . . I thought about how much Kumiko enjoyed dressing up—now we couldn't even go out and buy clothes together anymore.

Kumiko had once laughed so hard when she related to me a time that Katsumi had told her with pride, "Even a man like me can still be moved by the beauty of a flower." The big guy had said the exact same thing to me. When he'd said it I'd thought, *You say that but when you encounter something that's too beautiful for you, you just run away.*

Amiko and her husband came by to invite us to play tennis. They'd joined the new tennis club nearby. It was the first time I'd ever seen her husband in the bright morning light. He wasn't particularly tall or muscular in stature; in fact, he was rather short and stocky, yet his suntanned complexion and the way he carried himself implied that he was an all-around sportsman.

"We're both beginners. We'll just slow you down," I demurred, but Amiko's husband just laughed and reminded us about beginner's luck. When he smiled, his narrow eyes practically disappeared, but then at other times when he was looking closely at you or when he was talking seriously, suddenly his eyes would be piercing. He used "Amiko" when talking to his wife—unlike the big guy, he never called her "baby."

"Amiko plays Jomon tennis," Amiko's husband said.

"What is Jomon tennis like?" I asked.

"Nothing but running," he replied.

"That's good—running. In my case, I always mean to run but I can't get up any speed," I told him.

"This one only started playing about three years ago, so he can hardly talk," retorted Amiko.

I remembered Kumiko saying, "I found out that Katsumi used to work at a credit union. That's why he's always so unctuous. It's an occupational hazard, you know."

The big guy had never told me anything of his personal history. The Amikos were in the middle of a rally. Her husband would occasionally smack a return as if he were in the middle of a match, and she would yell at him.

There were six courts, all of them occupied. As there was no need to go off in pursuit of birds or animals, today's humans were chasing after little yellow balls instead. In place of sticks or spears, we ran around brandishing racquets. From time to time, we heard voices from the matches being played on the other courts.

Husbands and wives in all-white outfits, absorbed in hitting yellow balls back and forth.

Amiko had pretty good form, and she was fast, too. Her husband ran around on his sturdy legs. They were sportsman's legs, hard and muscular. Nothing pale or flabby about them.

The previous day's wind and rain seemed to have washed away any dirt and impurities, and the air and the sky were crystal clear. Into this perfect space, I longed to see the big guy dragged like a bull into some Spanish or Mexican bullfight, and then tortured to death. Well, he didn't have to die. I just wanted to watch him lumber around like a confused bull. To see him randomly shot at with yellow balls like bullets from a gun. He would start off grinning broadly, but soon enough the grin would be wiped from his face.

That big guy who used to say, "I can't play tennis or any of those elite sports," would be shot over and over with bouncing yellow bullets. There's no such thing as high-class or low-class sports. They're all just a way to pass the time. Whether it's tennis or golf, it's a way of killing a morning, or even a whole day, hitting balls around. Thanks to killing a half day or a whole day, you can reduce the total number of days in your lifetime by one.

The big guy's body is struck over and over by the yellow bullets, but there isn't a scratch on him, he's far from being killed. He's still grinning cheerfully and bowing obsequiously.

"You're taking this really seriously, Amiko," said her husband, wiping the sweat from his brow.

"I'm putting all my hatred into every shot," she replied with a grin.

"I wonder how it's possible to play such a strenuous sport in your old age. I half believed something I read that claimed you could play into your nineties, but now that I've given it a try myself, I'm beginning to think it's too demanding," I said.

"I'm guessing that if you're good at an early age then you're able to keep playing, at least a little, into old age," replied Amiko's husband, sipping from a can of soda.

Next, Amiko and I watched as the two men hit the ball around. "It's been too long. I'm out of shape," said Amiko. "Oh, by the way, I finally managed to get in touch with the man who used to be Kumiko's boyfriend. I told him what happened. Her death wasn't written up in the newspaper or anything, so it was the first time he'd heard about it. You know how Kumiko was always a little moody? Everyone thinks that it's only men who are sulky or obstinate. That's why nobody could ever understand someone like Kumiko. Her boyfriend was completely floored too. He just kept repeating over and over how strange it was, how he didn't understand it at all."

"Really? But I don't think Kumiko was that moody," I replied.

I'd lost sight of the big guy. I could no longer understand why I wanted to see him out on the tennis court to be mocked like something in a freak show. My aggression always seemed to be directed against the big guy. Hadn't it begun the very moment I saw him for the first time? Hadn't I, exhausted from all that aggression, begged Kumiko for help? And how had Kumiko dealt with the big guy? In a way, she'd been defeated by him, and eventually died. Kumiko had gone so far as to track down the information that he'd worked at a credit union. And also that, on quitting this credit union, he had gone to work as an accountant at N——Academy on the outskirts of H——City, just across the hill country. N——Academy was a small private school for children from elementary through high school. Apparently, it used to be the property of the massive N——Corporation. Kumiko suspected that there had been some sort of scandal; something that the big guy had got involved in at the credit union that had forced him to quit. He hadn't said anything specific but that was the impression that Kumiko had got. Kumiko seemed to have been sending me some kind of message that I had ignored. I'd failed to pick up any of the warning signals that Kumiko was giving off. I wondered whether the pronouncement that she wanted a child—if that had been some sort of signal too.

At Amiko's urging, I went out onto the court and hit the yellow ball. The ultimately futile impulse to beat the big guy to a pulp that had risen up in me now crashed like a wave. Like Hokusai's wave. Framed in the foamy arc of the wave, just like Mount Fuji in the original print, stands the big guy. In Hokusai's painting, a tiny boat, long and narrow in shape, has been scooped up like a leaf and is clinging to the crest of the wave. This precariously balanced, leaf-like boat is Kumiko. My wave crashes, failing to swallow up the big guy, but completely upending the little boat.

"Shall we do this again?" asked Amiko's husband, as we drank coffee together in the club house. Both our husband-and-wife pairs, silent as if overcome with a pleasant exhaustion, stared out blankly at the courts beyond the large bay windows. When I glanced at Amiko and her husband, it may have been the way the glaring sunlight fell on their faces, but it looked as if they were both crying.

"When the weather's this glorious, I just want to yell at the top of my lungs," said Amiko's husband, getting to his feet.

"I know what you mean. Let's all scream so loud they call an ambulance," I blurted.

Everyone laughed.

TAEKO TOMIOKA (1935–) gained recognition as a poet before turning to screenwriting, fiction, and essays. A prominent feminist writer, her work often questions the traditional roles of women and men in Japanese society. She was one of the screenwriters for the acclaimed film *Double Suicide*, and several of her short stories have appeared in English translation in *The Funeral of a Giraffe*.

LOUISE HEAL KAWAI holds an MA in Advanced Japanese Studies from the University of Sheffield. Originally from Manchester, England, she has lived in Nagoya, Japan, for about 20 years, teaching English language and literature. Her literary translations include short stories by Tamaki Daido and Taeko Kono as well as Shoko Tendo's best-selling autobiography, *Yakuza Moon*.

FORD MADOX FORD,
The March of Literature.
JON FOSSE, *Aliss at the Fire.*
Melancholy.
MAX FRISCH, *I'm Not Stiller.*
Man in the Holocene.
CARLOS FUENTES, *Christopher Unborn.*
Distant Relations.
Terra Nostra.
Vlad.
Where the Air Is Clear.
TAKEHIKO FUKUNAGA, *Flowers of Grass.*
WILLIAM GADDIS, *J R.*
The Recognitions.
JANICE GALLOWAY, *Foreign Parts.*
The Trick Is to Keep Breathing.
WILLIAM H. GASS, *Cartesian Sonata
and Other Novellas.*
Finding a Form.
A Temple of Texts.
The Tunnel.
Willie Masters' Lonesome Wife.
GÉRARD GAVARRY, *Hoppla! 1 2 3.*
Making a Novel.
ETIENNE GILSON,
The Arts of the Beautiful.
Forms and Substances in the Arts.
C. S. GISCOMBE, *Giscome Road.*
Here.
Prairie Style.
DOUGLAS GLOVER, *Bad News of the Heart.*
The Enamoured Knight.
WITOLD GOMBROWICZ,
A Kind of Testament.
PAULO EMÍLIO SALES GOMES, *P's Three
Women.*
KAREN ELIZABETH GORDON, *The Red Shoes.*
GEORGI GOSPODINOV, *Natural Novel.*
JUAN GOYTISOLO, *Count Julian.*
Exiled from Almost Everywhere.
Juan the Landless.
Makbara.
Marks of Identity.
PATRICK GRAINVILLE, *The Cave of Heaven.*
HENRY GREEN, *Back.*
Blindness.
Concluding.
Doting.
Nothing.
JACK GREEN, *Fire the Bastards!*
JIŘÍ GRUŠA, *The Questionnaire.*
GABRIEL GUDDING,
Rhode Island Notebook.
MELA HARTWIG, *Am I a Redundant
Human Being?*
JOHN HAWKES, *The Passion Artist.*
Whistlejacket.
ELIZABETH HEIGHWAY, ED., *Best of
Contemporary Fiction from Georgia.*
ALEKSANDAR HEMON, ED.,
Best European Fiction.
AIDAN HIGGINS, *Balcony of Europe.*
A Bestiary.
Blind Man's Bluff
Bornholm Night-Ferry.
Darkling Plain: Texts for the Air.
Flotsam and Jetsam.
Langrishe, Go Down.
Scenes from a Receding Past.
Windy Arbours.
KEIZO HINO, *Isle of Dreams.*
KAZUSHI HOSAKA, *Plainsong.*

ALDOUS HUXLEY, *Antic Hay.*
Crome Yellow.
Point Counter Point.
Those Barren Leaves.
Time Must Have a Stop.
NAOYUKI II, *The Shadow of a Blue Cat.*
MIKHAIL IOSSEL AND JEFF PARKER, EDS.,
*Amerika: Russian Writers View the
United States.*
DRAGO JANČAR, *The Galley Slave.*
GERT JONKE, *The Distant Sound.*
Geometric Regional Novel.
Homage to Czerny.
The System of Vienna.
JACQUES JOUET, *Mountain R.*
Savage.
Upstaged.
CHARLES JULIET, *Conversations with
Samuel Beckett and Bram van
Velde.*
MIEKO KANAI, *The Word Book.*
YORAM KANIUK, *Life on Sandpaper.*
HUGH KENNER, *The Counterfeiters.*
*Flaubert, Joyce and Beckett:
The Stoic Comedians.*
Joyce's Voices.
DANILO KIŠ, *The Attic.*
Garden, Ashes.
The Lute and the Scars
Psalm 44.
A Tomb for Boris Davidovich.
ANITA KONKKA, *A Fool's Paradise.*
GEORGE KONRÁD, *The City Builder.*
TADEUSZ KONWICKI, *A Minor Apocalypse.*
The Polish Complex.
MENIS KOUMANDAREAS, *Koula.*
ELAINE KRAF, *The Princess of 72nd Street.*
JIM KRUSOE, *Iceland.*
AYŞE KULIN, *Farewell: A Mansion in
Occupied Istanbul.*
EWA KURYLUK, *Century 21.*
EMILIO LASCANO TEGUI, *On Elegance
While Sleeping.*
ERIC LAURRENT, *Do Not Touch.*
HERVÉ LE TELLIER, *The Sextine Chapel.*
*A Thousand Pearls (for a Thousand
Pennies)*
VIOLETTE LEDUC, *La Bâtarde.*
EDOUARD LEVÉ, *Autoportrait.*
Suicide.
MARIO LEVI, *Istanbul Was a Fairy Tale.*
SUZANNE JILL LEVINE, *The Subversive
Scribe: Translating Latin
American Fiction.*
DEBORAH LEVY, *Billy and Girl.*
*Pillow Talk in Europe and Other
Places.*
JOSÉ LEZAMA LIMA, *Paradiso.*
ROSA LIKSOM, *Dark Paradise.*
OSMAN LINS, *Avalovara.*
The Queen of the Prisons of Greece.
ALF MAC LOCHLAINN,
The Corpus in the Library.
Out of Focus.
RON LOEWINSOHN, *Magnetic Field(s).*
MINA LOY, *Stories and Essays of Mina Loy.*
BRIAN LYNCH, *The Winner of Sorrow.*
D. KEITH MANO, *Take Five.*
MICHELINE AHARONIAN MARCOM,
The Mirror in the Well.
BEN MARCUS,
The Age of Wire and String.